"What will you do if I marry you?"

A little smile curved his lips. "Make slow, delectable love to you until—"

Heat scorching through her, she croaked, "I mean about Dad."

"As soon as he's my father-in-law, the business and the house will be his again."

"That's very generous," she said slowly.

"I'm sure you'll be worth it," Nick retorted sardonically.

"You don't really want me for a wife. You just want to use me as a...a sex object, to rid yourself of an obsession."

"Would you rather I said I loved you?"

LEE WILKINSON lives with her husband in a three-hundred-year-old stone cottage in Derbyshire, England, which gets cut off by snow most winters. They both enjoy traveling, and recently, joining forces with their daughter and son-in-law, spent a year going round the world "on a shoestring" while their son looked after Kelly, their much-loved German shepherd. Her hobbies are reading and gardening and holding impromptu barbecues for her long-suffering family and friends.

Books by Lee Wilkinson

HARLEQUIN PRESENTS®
1933—THE SECRET MOTHER
1991—A HUSBAND'S REVENGE

LEE WILKINSON

Wedding Fever

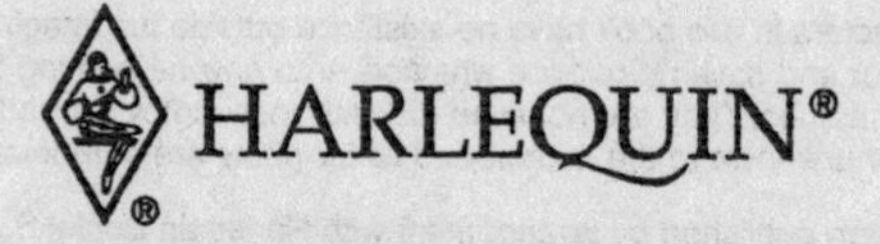

TORONTO • NEW YORK • LONDON
AMSTERDAM • PARIS • SYDNEY • HAMBURG
STOCKHOLM • ATHENS • TOKYO • MILAN • MADRID
PRAGUE • WARSAW • BUDAPEST • AUCKLAND

ISBN 0-373-12024-9

WEDDING FEVER

First North American Publication 1999.

This edition published by arrangement with Harlequin Books S.A.

Printed in U.S.A.

CHAPTER ONE

THE letter that was to turn Raine Marlowe's life upside down came out of the blue.

She and her father were eating breakfast in White Ladies' white-walled, black-beamed morning room. September sunshine, golden as honey, bathed the garden and poured in through the lattice windows.

Raine, blissfully unaware of the coming upheaval, was putting marmalade on her second piece of toast while Calib, as black and glossy as her own hair, his cat's eyes as green as her own, sat on the window-sill like a statue, the low sun gilding his fur and turning his whiskers to fine gold wire.

'Only one this morning,' the housekeeper announced cheerfully as she brought in the post.

Martha Deering had been with them twenty years and rated as one of the family.

'Thank you, Martha.'

Ralph, a nice-looking man with a rugged face and a thatch of iron-grey hair, accepted the letter. Finishing his coffee, he tore open the envelope, which bore a US stamp, and drew out the folded sheet of paper.

Glancing at her father's face as he read it, Raine saw that he looked shaken, tense. 'What is it?' she asked.

Taking of his horn-rimmed glasses, he said slowly, 'A letter from Harry.'

'Uncle Harry?'

'Yes.'

As he passed it to her a sudden presentiment made her shiver.

She knew that the twin brothers had quarrelled and lost touch long before she'd been born, though in their younger days they had been very close, and, after leaving college, had gone into the real estate business together.

Confirmed bachelors, and well on their way to being highly successful, they had both fallen in love with the same woman—a black-haired, green-eyed, gentle beauty named Lorraine, who had been Harry's girlfriend until she had met and fallen for his brother.

When, finally, she had agreed to marry Ralph, the brothers had split up. Ralph had kept White Ladies, the Elizabethan manor-house that had been the family home for generations, while Harry had realised enough capital to start another business and left for the States.

That had been almost thirty years ago.

The letter, which had a Boston address, was simple and to the point.

> No doubt it will seem strange hearing from me after all these years. I'm ashamed to admit that only pride has kept me from getting in touch sooner. I'm aware, through a family friend, that Lorraine died a long time ago, leaving only one daughter. My own wife has been dead for many years, and I'm alone except for my adopted son, Nick. I'm still on my feet, but my health has been a problem for some time now, and the specialist has finally confirmed that I only have a few months to live. I would dearly like to see you again before I die. Will you come over for a while and bring my niece? If she can forgive an old man for being so foolishly stubborn.

At the bottom was a postscript.

If you decide to come, please make it as soon as possible. The specialist may be out on his timing...

Green eyes grave, Raine looked up to ask, 'Will you be going?'

'Of course.' Her father answered without hesitation. 'What about you?'

'Do you want me to?'

'It would be a pity not to meet your uncle and cousin.'

'Then I'll come. If we can both be away together?'

Since leaving business college Raine had been her father's personal assistant. They went to work together each day; his office, in the little market town of Lopsley, was only ten minutes' drive from home.

'Certainly we can,' Ralph said, rising to his feet. 'Now, I'll go into the office and deal with that side of things while you make the travel arrangements.'

'When do you want to go?'

'Today, if possible. As soon as we're organised I'll ring Harry and let him know our time of arrival.'

Raine could tell by the barely suppressed urgency in her father's voice that all his old affection for his twin had come flooding back.

Some of that urgency rubbing off on her, she lost no time in phoning the airport, and in less than an hour they were booked on an evening flight to Boston.

The man waiting outside the international arrivals hall singled the pair out—a tall, spare, familiar-looking man accompanied by a slender black-haired beauty with wonderful Slavic cheekbones and a passionate mouth—and stepped forward.

Raine found herself looking up into a pair of long-lashed eyes the deep, dark blue of midnight—eyes of such a fascinating colour and shape that they took her breath away and made her heart do strange things.

They belonged to a tall, broad-shouldered man with a strong-boned face and thick, slightly curly hair the silvery-gold of ripe wheat.

'Raine Marlowe?' His voice was low and attractive, a little husky. Smiling at her surprise, increasing that electric sex-appeal by a thousand volts, he held out his hand. 'Nick.'

The feel of her fingers imprisoned by the lean strength of his made her tremble and sent the blood racing through her veins.

Turning to shake Ralph's hand, he said, 'I'd have known you anywhere. There's no mistaking the likeness between you and my father.'

While the two men dealt with the luggage and talked Raine tried not to stare at her cousin. Although she had been tipped off balance, she didn't want to stand gaping like some star-struck schoolgirl. But that tough, handsome face, that austere yet sensual mouth, those *eyes*, drew her gaze like a magnet.

'All set?' His question made her blink and look away hastily.

'All set,' she replied, and thought crossly that if she didn't pull herself together he'd put her down as a halfwit.

His sleek silver car was waiting, and as soon as he'd stowed their baggage they were off, heading into the heart of history-steeped Boston, the seventh largest city in the United States.

Indicating one of the elegant glass skyscrapers that filled the skyline, Nick remarked, 'That's where I have my offices.'

'Impressive,' Ralph commented. 'Harry mentioned that as well as running his companies you've been very successful on your own account. How difficult was it to build an international business empire before you were thirty?'

'Not difficult at all,' Nick answered coolly. 'The technique was, and is, simple but effective. I buy up ailing

businesses and reorganise them, cutting away the dead wood until they begin to make healthy growth...'

Raine had chosen to sit in the back, and while the men talked she stared out at the beautiful cosmopolitan city, which, though compact, had a wonderful feeling of airiness and space.

The skyline was full of contrasts. Tall skyscrapers and imposing modern buildings alternated with old steeples and clock towers and colonial landmarks.

It was a warm September evening, and as they drove towards Beacon Hill the streets seemed full of people strolling in summer dresses and short-sleeved shirts.

Red-brick mansions and narrow, gas-lit, cobblestoned streets gave the exclusive residential area, which sloped down to the Charles River, a picturesque, turn-of-the-century look.

The house Nick and his father shared was on Mecklenburg Place, one of the most elegant and charming squares, with tall shade trees and a central park. Illuminated by the streetlamps, the lacy canopy of leaves glowed with colour.

Number eight was a handsome, well-proportioned Georgian-style town-house, its front door flanked by symmetrical sash windows with rectangular panes and black-painted window-boxes full of autumn flowers.

As the car drew up outside the door it opened, spilling yellow light down the steps, and a tall, spare man with a rugged face and a thatch of iron-grey hair appeared.

Though Raine should have been prepared, it was oddly disconcerting to see a mirror image of her father.

Harry held out his hand.

Without a word, Ralph took it and wrung it. Then the two men were embracing, the warmth of their greeting wiping out the years of estrangement and separation as if they'd never been.

Raine, her eyes suspiciously bright, felt Nick's hand cup her elbow. They exchanged a look and a smile of under-

standing which brought them close mentally as well as physically.

Over the next week that feeling of closeness, of unspoken communication remained, and, instead of fading, Raine's first impression of Nick as the most wonderful man she'd ever met grew apace.

Apart from his stunning looks, she found that he was quick and brilliant and aware, with a strong character and a razor-sharp brain.

A conversation she overheard between the brothers one day proved that as well as loving him, his adoptive father respected him.

'No one can afford to be soft in business,' Ralph was saying. 'There's too many sharks about.'

'You're right,' Harry agreed, and added, 'Nick's far from soft. Not many try to cheat or hoodwink him. The few who do, don't last long.'

'But he seems to be a good employer?'

'He won't keep anyone who's unnecessary or who doesn't pull his weight, but he cares about people. I've known him sack a man for being lazy then out of his own pocket support that man's family until he's found another job...'

From the first Raine had sensed a certain ruthlessness in Nick, and, falling deeper under his spell, *wanting* to think well of him, she was gladdened by that glimpse of humanity.

Every day she discovered more about his complex personality, about the man as a whole, and she liked what she found.

As well as an athletic build and a striking face—redeemed from film-star handsomeness by a strong nose and jaw—he had a kind of magnetism, a natural arrogance which made most women give him a second and lingering look.

Yet he was totally lacking in vanity or any kind of con-

ceit, and, though he was quite capable of being hard and despotic, he was also caring and generous, with no petty faults or meanness of spirit.

He had everything and more that she had ever dared hope to find in a man, and, though she did her best to hide it beneath a cheerful camaraderie, the fascination he exerted intensified until he filled her thoughts by day and her dreams by night.

But she had no idea how he felt about her.

Often, when her eyes were drawn irresistibly to his face, she found he was studying her, but his cool expression gave nothing away and it was impossible to guess what he was thinking.

He took a vacation from the office and the four of them walked the Freedom Trail, saw the US Constitution, marvelled at the shimmering reflection of Trinity Church in the soaring glass of Hancock Tower, visited the Omni Theater at the Museum of Science and ate lunch in bustling Quincy Market.

With the unspoken knowledge that time was running out, they packed as much into their days as possible, and each night—after Raine had gone to bed and Nick had retired to his study to catch up on some work—the two brothers sat talking until the early hours of the morning.

One night, leaving the older men to their endless reminiscing, Nick followed Raine up the elegant staircase.

Talking casually, they paused by her bedroom door. She was smiling at something he'd said, when suddenly he bent and kissed her gently—then not gently at all.

The universe exploded in a flash of fire that was followed by a darkness like folds of thick black velvet.

When his lips had reluctantly freed themselves, he said huskily, 'Goodnight, Raine. Sleep well.'

Closing the door of her room behind her, she leaned weakly against the panels and knew that her life would never be the same again.

That night she dreamt of white lace and orange blossom,

of rice and rose petals and stained-glass windows, of living happily ever afterwards…

Next day, not being one to wear her heart on her sleeve, she did her best to maintain her usual veneer of composure. But Raine—cool, self-contained, *sensible* Raine—was head over heels in love, and happiness and excitement fizzed and bubbled inside her like champagne.

When, after a morning walk on the common, the four returned to Mecklenburg Place, Mrs Espling, the housekeeper, had a message from Nick's secretary. Some business had cropped up that demanded his attention.

That evening, returning from the office in time to have a meal with them, Nick seemed unusually quiet and thoughtful.

While the two older men talked, Nick ate in silence. Raine watched him surreptitiously from beneath long lashes.

She was studying the planes and angles of that hard, lean face, the wide, mobile mouth, the strong nose and the well-marked brows, several shades darker than the thick blond hair, when he looked up and saw her.

Afraid the longing she felt was only too visible, she flushed scarlet and bent her head, allowing her black silky hair to partially curtain her face.

'I have to go up to Maine tomorrow,' Nick remarked during a lull in the conversation.'

'Maine?' Ralph raised an eyebrow.

Harry answered. 'Donkey's years ago I bought a lumber company and several paper mills up there. Nick takes time from his own business affairs to look after them for me.'

Nick smiled. 'An occasional trip to Maine is no hardship. It's a wild, beautiful state, well worth a visit. How about if we all go?'

Harry shook his head. 'I'm afraid you'll have to count me out.'

'What's it like?' Ralph asked his nephew.

'Lakes, mountains, a spectacular rocky coastline with

hundreds of small islands, charming little towns, white clapboard churches, quaint fishing villages, hidden harbours and colourful lighthouses… A lot of the sparse population live near the coast and make their living from the sea.

'Northeast, towards Canada, is the Allagash—a wilderness of forests and swamps and waterways, where most of the logging is done.'

'Sounds marvellous,' Ralph said, 'but I think I'll stick with Boston.'

'Why don't you two young ones go?' Harry suggested.

'How about it, Raine?' Midnight-blue eyes caught and held green.

A trip alone with Nick would be as exhilarating as jumping out of a plane at thirty thousand feet without a parachute—and as dangerous.

'I'd love to,' she said, and if he noticed the quiver in her voice, hopefully he would put it down to excitement.

The next day they caught an early flight up to Bangor. Then Nick, piloting the company's small plane, which had been specially fitted with dual landing gear—wheels and floats—and extra fuel tanks, took them to the Maine wilderness.

They were to visit the site offices of the lumber company, and landed on a graded road, following a huge truck piled high with massive tree trunks held in place by chains.

Seeing that Raine was startled, Nick told her, 'There are no airstrips out here. Either we land on water, or on one of these logging roads that belong to the company.'

He steered the plane over uneven ground and they bumped through enormous wire mesh gates and into a kind of compound, where there were several long prefabricated buildings.

Climbing the steps to what was obviously the office block, they were greeted by a short, plump, balding man, wearing a hairy checked shirt and rimless glasses. Nick addressed him as Elmo.

Raine was ushered to a hard wooden chair and plied with strong black coffee and thick slices of cake while Nick sorted out the problem that had taken him there.

Business completed, he returned to say casually, 'We have a log cabin over at Owl Creek. Would you like to stay there for a few days and see something of the backwoods? Or would you prefer to go somewhere more civilised?'

Without hesitation, she burnt her bridges. 'Oh, stay at Owl Creek.'

They flew over forests of spruce, fir, pine and birch, interlaced with gleaming waterways, and landed on the mirror-like surface of Owl Lake, disturbing its evening cloud reflections.

Ringed by hills clothed in the scarlet and gold, green and bronze of ash and maple, tamarack and cedar, it was the most beautiful place Raine had ever seen.

The substantially built, single-storey log cabin was on the lakeshore about half a mile from Owl Creek. Set well back from the water, it was in the centre of a wide clearing and raised on piles, with an open veranda running along three sides and a screened porch.

Nick opened the heavy door, and, having stooped to put a match to the stove, left her to look around while he brought their luggage from the plane.

The kitchenette was fairly basic. Apart from a sink and an old-fashioned hand-operated washing machine, it had a gas cooker, which was connected, and a gas fridge, which wasn't. But the larder was stocked with all manner of dried and tinned goods, including tins of butter and malted brown bread.

Beyond the kitchenette was a small, separate bedroom and next to that a bathroom—luxurious, Raine guessed, by backwoods standards—with a porcelain sink and bath, a shower cabinet and a flush toilet.

But most of the space was taken up by a large, attractive, open-plan room on split levels.

The living area was simply furnished with two long bookcases, a coffee-table and a comfortable black leather suite. There were boldly patterned cushions and curtains, and matching Aztec-type mats were scattered on the polished wooden floor. The huge wood-burning stove stood in a stone fireplace, and in front of it lay a shaggy bearskin rug.

To one side, on a curved, slightly raised dais, were a stripped pine wardrobe, a dressing-table, a blanket chest and a large divan.

The air was cold and held the faint mustiness of a place that had been shut up for some time, but already crackling flames were devouring the kindling and licking around the pile of split logs in the stove.

'Like it?' Nick asked as he carried in their cases.

'Love it,' she answered lightly, trying to ignore the tension between them—a sexual tension which had been growing ever since she'd agreed to come here. 'Incidentally, the bathroom surprised me.'

He grinned briefly. 'I'm old enough to prefer a certain standard of comfort.'

'But how do you manage it?'

'The water's pumped from a well, and bottled gas provides heating and lighting. Speaking of which…'

Dusk was falling rapidly, and, after bending to light a taper, Nick touched it to the gas mantles, which lit with little plops and blossomed into yellow flowers. That done, he drew the heavy curtains over the windows, making the place cosy and intimate.

'I'll cook tonight,' he said. 'Your turn tomorrow. But first we'll have a drink.'

While she stood by the stove, enjoying the blaze, he brought a bottle of Chablis from the larder, and, having opened it, poured two glasses and handed one to her.

As she accepted it his fingers brushed hers, and she caught her breath audibly.

Their eyes met and held. Something deep and primitive flared in his—a look that was at once a challenge and a statement of intent.

She knew without a shadow of doubt that if she didn't want him, now was the time to make that plain. All she had to do was break eye contact and step back.

But she *did* want him—with a passion that made her blood run through her veins as hot and impatient as molten lava. Green eyes drowned in blue, she took a step forward.

Removing the glass from her nerveless fingers, he set it carefully on the table.

But, instead of leading her to the bed, he laid her down in front of the stove with a cushion beneath her dark head, and, stretching out beside her, kissed her eyes and her throat and her mouth with a passionate hunger that turned her very bones to water.

She was his to take then, and he must have known that, but, keeping his own desire leashed, slowly, unhurriedly, with enjoyment and finesse, he set out to rouse hers to fever-pitch.

The fire-glow gilded her creamy skin as he slowly undressed her, savouring each new discovery, erotically exploring her exquisite, sensuous body with eyes and hands and mouth.

High, perfectly shaped breasts with dusky nipples firmed enticingly to his touch, offering themselves as tempting morsels for a hungry mouth. A slender waist asked to be stroked and spanned by two strong hands. Curving hips invited leaner hips to fit into their seductive cradle.

'You're the most beautiful woman I've ever seen,' he told her huskily as he stripped off his own clothes. 'You enchant me.'

Her body responded to his without shame, arching to his touch, welcoming him, holding nothing back.

He was a skilful, considerate lover, and, though she was

a virgin, there was no pain, only a joyous acceptance and a growing, spiralling delight that finally ended in a climax so intense that she felt as if her body had imploded into a white-hot core of pure sensation.

She was lying in his arms, her head on his shoulder, her heartbeat and breathing slowly returning to normal, when he queried softly, 'First time, Raine?'

Wondering if he preferred experienced women, she asked, a shade hesitantly, 'Do you mind?'

'Mind? I feel like a king!'

After that first rapturous coming together they made love morning, noon and night, as though they were on their honeymoon, leaving the bed they shared only to shower or to eat, to take an occasional walk or a canoe trip on the lake.

Nick called her, 'My green-eyed witch,' and told her how lovely she was and how much he wanted her.

He never said the three words Raine was longing to hear, but it was only a matter of time, she felt sure—just an initial reluctance to admit to the deepest and most binding human emotion of all.

Neither wanted that idyllic week to end, but when, all too soon, the weekend came, he sighed and said they had to return.

They got an early start. During the journey home Nick seemed silent and abstracted, but, transported by love, Raine travelled back to Boston on cloud nine, deliriously happy with the present, glowingly confident about the future.

On reaching Mecklenburg Place, they found that Harry and Ralph had gone to a ball game and that an urgent message from Nick's secretary was waiting.

'Damn!' he muttered, frowning. 'I need to talk to you—to tell you something—but I'd better go into the office first. There are some important papers I have to look through and sign.'

Taking both her hands in his, he gave them a squeeze. 'I shouldn't be more than a couple of hours at the most. Will you be all right on your own?'

'Of course.' She smiled at his concern.

He claimed her mouth in a hard, almost savage kiss, and, before she could even kiss him back, he was gone.

Wondering what he wanted to tell her, hoping she *knew*, she went up to her room and unpacked the small case she'd taken to Maine, blushing a little to think how few clothes she'd worn for most of the time—how few *either* of them had worn.

She was on her way back to the big, sunny living room when Mrs Espling appeared in the hall and asked pleasantly, 'Can I get you anything, Miss Marlowe? A tray of tea, perhaps?'

'Oh, thank you. That would be lovely.'

Raine was just pouring a second cup and finishing one of the housekeeper's delicious blueberry muffins when, without warning, the door burst open.

Looking up, a glad smile on her lips, she was surprised to see a slender, dark-haired woman, perhaps a year or two older than herself.

'Hi!' the newcomer said cheerfully. 'I'm Tina. You must be Nick's cousin. When he spoke to me on the phone he told me you and your father were coming over... Is he home?'

'No, he's gone into the office.'

'On a Saturday!' The bright brown eyes clouded with disappointment. 'Any idea how long he'll be?'

'He said possibly a couple of hours.'

'Then I'll have plenty of time to go home and unpack.'

'Do you live far away?' Raine asked politely.

'Just next door—' Tina dropped into the nearest chair, obviously quite at home '—so I'm used to seeing Nick most days. Now it seems *ages* since I saw him—and gosh have I missed him!'

Then, by way of explanation, she went on, 'For the last

three weeks I've been staying in New York with an old schoolfriend. I've only just this minute got back. Nick was coming to the airport to meet me, only the—' She broke off abruptly, then went on, 'Only I found I could get home a day earlier than I'd expected, so I decided to surprise him.'

She was pushing back a stray dark curl when Raine noticed the sparkling sapphire on her left hand, and, with a sudden premonition, she remarked through stiff lips, 'What a beautiful ring.'

Tina's pretty pale face lit up. 'Yes, isn't it? I wanted a diamond solitaire, but Nick said it wasn't my style and he chose this one.'

Feeling as though she was being shut in an iron maiden, Raine asked, 'How long have you been engaged?'

'Nick proposed to me and we went to buy the ring the day before I left for New York.'

Getting to her feet, Tina headed for the door. 'I'll go and unpack his present. I bought him a watch from Tiffany's. I want it to be a surprise, so if he gets back before I do, don't tell him.'

'I won't be seeing him,' Raine said, and it was a prayer. Her voice controlled, even, she added, 'Something's cropped up and I need to go home, so I'll be off to the airport myself in a minute or two.'

'Well, so long, then.' Tina gave her a wide, friendly smile. 'I hope you've enjoyed your visit. Have a good journey home.'

As soon as the door had closed behind the slim figure Raine phoned for a taxi. Then, hurrying upstairs, she threw her belongings into her suitcase with desperate haste, scrawled a note for her father, telling him that she was needed at home because Martha was poorly, and one for her uncle, thanking him for all his kindness, and was outside waiting as the cab drew up.

Luck was with her and she managed to get a seat on a plane that was leaving for London within the hour.

Throughout the flight she sat pale and tense, dry-eyed, though her heart wept tears of blood.

Once a concerned stewardess touched her shoulder and asked, 'Are you feeling ill? Can I get you anything?'

Grateful for the kindness, Raine shook her head and said, 'No, I'm fine, thank you. Just tired.'

Tired and bitter and disillusioned, and swamped by such pain that, unable to bear it, she struggled to whip up anger to take its place.

What a fool she'd been. What a blind, stupid fool! All he'd wanted was a little light dalliance, some casual sex while his fiancée was away, but she'd given him everything she had to give—her heart as well as her body.

And how eagerly she'd offered *that*. Responding with a passionate sensuality she hadn't realised she was capable of. She'd acted like a wanton.

And what if she was pregnant? Pregnant by a man who had only wanted an easy exchange of pleasure with no commitments. A sophisticated man who had no doubt presumed that *she* had taken precautions.

Horror filled her, causing her entire body to flush with heat. She felt her face and throat burn and a trickle of perspiration run down between her breasts.

A feverish calculation reassured her that her stupidity was unlikely to have dire results.

Aware of just how much the knowledge of her behaviour would upset her father, she felt sick with relief. Now he would never need to know.

Though that was pure luck. She flayed herself with the thought. Nothing could alter the fact that she had behaved like the worst kind of fool. A fool who had given in to passion, presuming that because she loved Nick he must love her, and that marriage and a home and family would automatically follow.

But she'd learnt a painful, mortifying lesson and learnt it well. Never, *never* again would she allow passion to rule her.

* * *

She had scarcely arrived home when a phone call from her father, enquiring how Martha was, threw her into a panic. Unused to lying, she found herself stammering, 'Sh-she doesn't seem too bad…'

'What's wrong?'

'I'm not sure… Some kind of flu…'

'Then you can cope? You don't need me back?'

'Of course not.'

'How did you manage at such short notice?'

Doing her best to sound her normal self, Raine endeavoured to answer her father's questions and allay his concern.

'Well, don't try to go into work as well as taking care of Martha,' he said eventually.

'I'll see how things are,' she hedged.

'And let me know if you need me.'

'I'm sure I won't. I'd much rather you stayed with Uncle Harry… Give him my love.'

'Don't go,' Ralph said. 'Nick's waiting to speak to you…'

'Raine…'

She heard the urgency in the deep voice as, trembling in every limb, she put the phone down.

Common sense told her it would have been better to speak to him, to pretend, for her pride's sake, that the little incident had meant nothing to her. But she knew only too well that she would have been unable to hide her pain and misery, her humiliation and shame.

The next weeks were the worst of her life. Feeling as though she was slowly bleeding to death, Raine somehow struggled through the long days and even longer nights.

Martha, having been told only that Raine had needed an excuse to come home, looked at her with anxious eyes, but, never one to pry, said nothing.

Nick tried several times to ring her, but Raine refused

to speak to him, and, recognising his bold scrawl, destroyed the letters he sent unopened.

She went back to the office and tried to lose herself in her work, but the thought of Nick was always at the back of her mind, and a black weight of emptiness lay on her spirit.

She missed him and longed for him constantly, even while she reminded herself that he was hard and callous and uncaring—that he'd not only used her but betrayed his fiancée.

Ralph was reluctant to leave his brother, and it was a month before he came home. Though Raine was still fighting a desolation of spirit so intense that she felt she would never recover, she was able to hide it better by then, and met her father's shrewd eyes with relative composure.

When, apart from asking how Harry was, she avoided mentioning Boston, Ralph took the bull by the horns. 'What did you and Nick quarrel about?'

'What makes you think we quarrelled?'

'Don't take me for a fool, girl. I know you've been refusing to speak to him, and, though Martha did her best, she's no better at lying than you are.'

When Raine said nothing, her father went on, 'It must have been something pretty serious to send you running home like a scalded cat, but I'm sure—'

'Please, Dad,' she broke in desperately. 'I don't want to talk about it.'

Seeing her set face, the stubborn line of her mouth, he sighed. 'Perhaps you'll change your mind when Nick comes over.'

Feeling as though she'd been punched in the solar plexus, she croaked, 'Over *here*? When is he coming?'

'He said as soon as he can get away. Probably this weekend.'

CHAPTER TWO

AFTER a night spent tossing and turning, and with her mind finally made up, Raine rose early and pushed a few necessities into a case. That done, she wrote a note to her father saying that she was going up to London for a few days, then, while the household still slept, she quietly let herself out.

No doubt it was cowardly, but she couldn't bear to stay and face Nick. Whatever it was that was bringing him here—a pricking conscience? Belated guilt at not having told her he had a fiancée?—she didn't want to know.

Nothing he could say or do would wipe out the past or mitigate her shame. Seeing him again, hearing him apologise, would only add unbearably to her humiliation, strip away any remaining shreds of self-respect.

It was a dark, chilly November morning, with mist lying over the herbaceous borders and shrouding the trees, and, feeling like a fugitive, she hurried down to the old stable block that many years previously had been converted into garages.

The engine of her small car sprang into life immediately, and, its lights feeling the mist like the antennae of some insect, she drove down the drive and turned left towards the station.

Leaving the car in the station car park, she caught the early train into town. By breakfast-time she was booked into a quiet hotel near Green Park, confident that she could safely lose herself in London until Nick had given up and gone back to the States.

Over the next few days she did her level best not to think about him, but the memories refused to be banished completely.

Whenever she relaxed her guard she recalled the smile in his voice when he spoke to her, the way his eyes crinkled at the corners when he smiled at her, the swift mental affinity which had made them enjoy each other's company so much… And a great deal more she would rather have forgotten.

And *would* forget, she vowed. She wouldn't let herself keep on recalling the past, thinking of a man who belonged to another woman. A man who had only wanted to use her.

Knowing it would drive her mad to sit in her room, she forced herself to go out each day—walking, window-shopping, visiting museums and art galleries, passing the time somehow, *anyhow*, until she could go home.

On the fifth day of her self-imposed exile her phone call to White Ladies shook her, making her drop the receiver as though it were red-hot when Nick's deep voice answered.

Though she had no appetite, she made herself eat, and at night, refusing to let herself brood, she went to concerts, to the opera and to a couple of the long-running shows.

Leaving the theatre on Friday night, after seeing a musical, she found that it was raining. Rather then just stand being jostled by the crowd, she had started to walk down Shaftesbury Avenue, keeping her eye open for a taxi, when she cannoned into a tall, slimly built man hurrying the opposite way.

The impact made her step back and drop her clutch-bag, which opened, spilling its contents all over the wet pavement.

'I'm so sorry,' the well-dressed stranger apologised, and, stooping, he began to gather up her belongings and drop them back into her bag.

Thanking him, she admitted, 'It was my fault. I was

trying to find a taxi and not looking where I was going.' As she spoke she put weight on her right foot and winced.

'Is there something wrong?' he asked, his voice clear, with a distinctly upper-class accent.

'I've just stepped awkwardly and turned my ankle. It's nothing serious.'

'Can you walk?'

'Oh, yes.' She took a step to prove it, and winced again.

His look held concern. 'Perhaps I'd better give you a lift. My car's quite close.'

When she hesitated, he added, 'You won't stand much chance of finding a taxi on a night like this.'

He was young and good-looking, with gold-rimmed glasses and a reassuring air of quiet respectability.

'Well, if it's not out of your way...' she said slowly. 'I'm staying at the Wirral Hotel, near Green Park.'

'I know it. And it's not out of my way. I have a flat in Curzon Street, and the family home is in Mayfair.'

'Then, thank you. It's very kind of you.'

'Not at all,' he said politely, meaninglessly, as he offered her his arm with old-fashioned courtesy. As they began to walk—Raine hobbling slightly—he added, 'My name's Kevin...Kevin Somersby.'

'Raine Marlowe.'

'Raine?' he echoed blankly.

'Short for Lorraine,' she explained.

'Oh.' Judging from his frown, he didn't approve of shortening names.

His car was an extension of himself—an expensive, well-polished, rather sober saloon. He handed her in with care, and she found herself thinking that his excellent manners must have been instilled from birth.

During the short drive they chatted, and it came as no surprise to discover that he worked in the Foreign Office and that his mother was Lady Maude Somersby.

Though he was handsome, it was in an oddly negative way. His looks didn't raise her blood pressure one iota, and he was so prosaic that he neither stimulated nor disturbed her. In short, he presented no threat, and she found herself relaxing in his company.

Having escorted her into the hotel lobby and been duly thanked, he wished her a pleasant goodnight.

'Goodnight...and thank you again.' Raine offered him her hand.

He held it for a moment, then asked a shade diffidently, 'May I call tomorrow to enquire how the ankle is?'

'Of course.'

He was a very nice, correct young man, she thought as she took the lift up to her room, and the complete antithesis of Nick.

When Kevin turned up after breakfast next morning, with a dozen long-stemmed roses and an invitation to lunch, she had no hesitation in accepting.

The lunch-date stretched into the afternoon, and they ended up having dinner and spending the evening together.

Before leaving her that night, he asked hopefully how long she would be staying in town.

Telling herself that Nick would surely get the message and go home soon, she answered vaguely, 'I'm not sure...probably another day or two.'

Clearly crestfallen, Kevin rallied to ask, 'will you come to Manton Square tomorrow for lunch? Mother would like to meet you.'

Not sure how she could get out of going, and not even sure that she *wanted* to, Raine answered politely, 'Thank you, I'd love to.'

'Then I'll pick you up about twelve.' Kevin looked relieved, and Raine felt a sudden conviction that the invitation had been issued so that she could be vetted as a suitable companion for Lady Somersby's only son.

Such was the case.

The next day she found herself greeted with the utmost courtesy by a regal lady with a cast-iron hairdo, several strings of pearls and pale eyes like gimlets.

After an excellent lunch, having been politely but minutely grilled about her background and social standing, Raine was given what was evidently the seal of approval when Lady Somersby suggested that Kevin might take her to see the family portraits.

The following evening, after a phone call to Martha had reassured her that Nick had returned to the States, Raine told Kevin she would be going home the next day. His obvious disappointment was somewhat alleviated when she added, 'You'll be very welcome at White Ladies any time you care to call.'

'Have you a car in town?' he queried.

'No, I came by train.'

'Then perhaps I could drive you home?'

'That's very kind of you,' she said automatically, 'but won't you be at your office?'

'I have some days due to me,' he announced firmly.

Raine found herself wondering what her father would think when she arrived home with a strange man in tow. But after some consideration she decided it was the ideal solution. Kevin's presence would prove that she wasn't mooning over Nick, and it should help to smooth over what might otherwise have been an uncomfortable homecoming.

Safe in the knowledge that no matter how vexed he was with her, her father would be polite and pleasant to any guest, she suggested, 'If you have nothing planned for the evening, perhaps you'll stay for dinner?'

Kevin gave her his charming smile. 'Thank you, I'd like to.'

From then on he became a constant visitor, and early in the spring, with due ceremony, he proposed to her.

Raine had seen it coming, and she didn't need to think about it. With Kevin, everything would be ordered and placid. *He* would never tear her apart emotionally and leave her bleeding to death. It might not be the most exciting of marriages, but they were happy and comfortable together. They wanted the same things out of life.

She said yes.

He bought her a discreet diamond solitaire and they began planning the wedding and their future together. In the following months there were only two things they disagreed on—working wives and where to live.

Raine wanted to continue with her job, at least for a time, but Kevin proved to be unexpectedly obdurate about it.

The contentious topics were shelved several times, and then, on Friday evening in September, as they strolled through the garden at White Ladies, Kevin reintroduced them.

'It's time we came to a decision, old thing,' he said, and then, almost as though it clinched matters, 'I have to tell you that Mother strongly disapproves of these modern marriages where the wife keeps working to the detriment of family life. And in any case,' he continued, 'my flat is too far away to make commuting every day feasible.'

'I'd rather hoped not to have to leave Dad,' Raine replied. 'He's looked after me ever since Mum died, and I'm all he's got.'

Seeing Kevin frown, she added persuasively, 'There's a large, self-contained apartment here at White Ladies, and, with your office situated where it is, it wouldn't be any further for *you* to travel to work than you're travelling now.'

But once again he was adamant. 'I've always felt that a wife should move into her husband's home, not the other way around.'

'But what would I *do* all day, cooped up in a London flat?'

His pale grey eyes looked hurt. 'I hope we'll entertain quite a bit when we're married, and there's voluntary work and committees and things… Mother will be pleased to help and advise you. And we've agreed we want to start a family.'

She seized on that. 'Surely a town flat isn't the ideal place to bring up children?'

'When the time comes we'll look for a house in the country,' he promised. 'Agreed?'

She nodded, and said reluctantly, 'Very well. I'll tell Dad I won't be going back to work after the wedding.'

Having got what he wanted, Kevin was willing to be gracious. 'If you'd like to be close to your father, when we do buy a house we can try to find something within a reasonable distance of White Ladies as well as London.'

He kissed her cheek. 'I must go. I'm taking Mother to a charity function in the morning and then on to lunch, but I should be here some time in the afternoon. By the way, we'll be dining in Lopsley. I've booked a table at that new place you said you wanted to try.'

Disarmed by his thoughtfulness, his attempt to please her, she accompanied him to the door and waved him off.

The old walled garden was a suntrap. Eyes closed, head pillowed on her discarded woolly, Raine lay flat on her back on the smooth, green expanse of turf in the centre while she waited for her fiancé.

The late afternoon sun shone redly through her eyelids. She could hear the bees buzzing around the lavender and autumn roses, and smell the various pungent herbs. A baby breeze patted her cheek and ruffled her wispy half-fringe.

Calib sat on her stomach, blinking sleepily while he contemplated nothing in particular. Applying a pink tongue to a velvet paw, he began to wash leisurely behind one ear.

His hearing was more acute than his human companion's, and he looked up and paused in his ablutions a second or two before the door in the high pink-brick wall opened.

Raine heard the steps cross the crazy-paving path that meandered past the flower-borders, and felt Calib's easy spring as he abandoned his perch. He always absented himself when Kevin came, determinedly repulsing all his attempts to make friends.

Her fiancé's shadow falling over her face momentarily blotted out the sun. Keeping her eyes shut, she murmured a lazy hello, and smiled a little invitation.

When he sat down beside her and leaned over to let his mouth lightly brush hers, she reached up to put her arms around his neck.

Rather to her surprise she felt him stretch out beside her. Normally Kevin wasn't one for lying about on the grass. Even the touch of his lips seemed different. Less deferential. More disturbing. *Much* more disturbing.

All thought was suspended as, making her heart start to race with suffocating speed and sending a swift surge of pleasure through her, he deepened the kiss.

While her entire body sang into life and a core of liquid heat formed in the pit of her stomach he explored her mouth with masterful thoroughness, one hand following the curve of her hip and buttock in a way it had never done before.

A sudden fear, like the shock of an icy plunge, made her brain click into gear.

Until now, Nick had been the only man who had ever been able to engender such an urgent and overwhelming response. And she didn't want to feel this way. It terrified her.

Stiffening in rejection, she tried to push him away.

Refusing to be so summarily dismissed, he finished the kiss unhurriedly before lifting his head.

Raine's eyes flew open.

At first, dazzled by the low sun, she could see nothing but brightness. Then she found herself focusing on a lean, sardonic face, with brows and lashes several shades darker than the thick blond hair, and eyes of a deep midnight-blue. A strong-boned, handsome face. No, much more than handsome—a fascinating, *compelling* face. A face she had taught herself to hate. A face she'd hoped never to see again...

Panic swept over her as her worst fears were confirmed. '*You*!' she whispered, jerking upright. Trying to swamp fear with anger, she demanded furiously, 'What are you doing here? How dare you kiss me like that?'

A level brow was lifted mockingly. 'How did you want me to kiss you?' His mouth, the top lip thin, the bottom one seductive, was much too close for comfort. 'With more respect and less enthusiasm, as I understand your noble fiancé does?'

'I don't want you to kiss me at all,' she hissed at him.

'You did once,' he reminded her with deliberate cruelty.

Her mind was suddenly in confusion, beset by memories that returned to her with devastating clarity.

Calib, who had been watching from a short distance away, came back with a little rush to push between them as, face burning, Raine ignored the goad and demanded, 'And how do *you* know how Kevin kisses me?'

'Your father described Kevin Somersby as a minor civil servant—a steady and correct young man.'

'Which you interpreted as dull and inhibited!'

Rising to his feet in one fluid movement, Nick held out a lean suntanned hand. 'Was I wrong?'

'Totally wrong! He's—' Breaking off the hasty words, she said coldly, 'I've no intention of discussing Kevin with you.' Carefully avoiding Nick's outstretched hand, she scrambled to her feet.

The clamour of her own heartbeat almost deafening her, she busied herself brushing wisps of grass from her grey and white striped cotton shirtwaister.

Her diamond solitaire flashed in the sun. Aware that his eyes followed it thoughtfully, she asked again, 'What are you *doing* here?'

His healthy white teeth gleamed in a smile. A smile that, like his words, held a subtle threat. 'If the mountain won't come to Mahomet...'

Just for an instant both her heart and breathing seemed to stop. She took a long, shuddering breath and asked the first thing that came into her head. 'Did Dad know you were coming?'

'Yes, he knew. I gather he didn't tell you?'

Her green eyes flashed. 'You probably asked him not to!'

Neither confirming nor denying the charge, Nick said, 'I thought it was high time we had a talk.'

Feeling as though a silken noose was tightening around her throat, she informed him, 'There's nothing to talk about. I'm going to be married in a month.' She spoke the words as though they were a talisman with the power to keep danger at bay.

'Really?' he drawled.

'Yes, really.' She strove to sound serene and certain, but all at once she hardly believed it herself. To add substance to the declaration, and aware that her father and Nick corresponded regularly, she added, 'Surely Dad must have mentioned it?' And then she knew that of course he had. That was why Nick was here!

His smile oblique, Nick agreed, 'Oh, yes, he *mentioned* it...' But he wasn't very happy about it. The words were as clear as if they'd been spoken aloud. Eyes glinting, Nick went on, 'However, I gather he doesn't think too much of your intended.'

It was the truth and she couldn't deny it. Angry with both of them, she said sharply, 'What he thinks of Kevin is nothing to do with you.'

'Oh, I don't know... Apart from anything else we're family. Kissing cousins, you might say.'

When Raine failed to rise to the bait, stooping to stroke Calib, who, purring like a young traction engine, was winding sinuously around Nick's ankles, he remarked reflectively, 'Though, apart from just now, it's almost a year since you last kissed me.'

Swallowing hard, feeling the past she'd struggled so

hard to leave behind closing in on her, Raine denied it. 'I didn't kiss you just now.'

Straightening to his full height of well over six feet, towering over her five feet six inches, he said, 'Strange. That's what it felt like.'

'I thought it was Kevin.'

'Well, if he's able to make you respond so passionately, perhaps your father's wrong about him being prudish.'

Though she knew he was trying to provoke her, she couldn't stop herself saying, 'Kevin's not prudish. He just isn't—' Breaking off, she continued raggedly, 'I much prefer romance to...'

'Passion?' Nick suggested when she faltered. Dark blue eyes holding an expression that could have been contempt, he continued derisively, 'But of course romance is so much less disturbing than passion—less of a risk. Holding hands, a stroll in the moonlight, a chaste kiss—that doesn't demand any real commitment, any great depth of feeling. Everything's calm and orderly and *safe*.'

He was a fine one to talk about commitment, about depth of feeling. Desperately she fought back. 'If that's how I want things to be it still has nothing to do with you.'

'*Why* do you want things to be that way?'

Because surrendering to passion had almost destroyed her, and she had no intention of ever letting it happen again.

When, staring blindly at a magnificent display of orange dahlias, she failed to answer Nick's question, he took her shoulders and made her look at him. '*Why*, Raine? *Why* do you want things to be calm and orderly and safe? It doesn't seem to be much of a recipe for marriage. It's like trying to sail a three-masted schooner on a pond rather than taking it out to sea.'

She made an attempt to pull herself away and felt a rush of relief when he let her go. 'Some people get seasick.'

'Kevin, for instance?'

'It suits us both to have a calm, friendly—'

'*Friendly*! Ye gods...a platonic marriage.'

On the defensive, she cried, 'It won't be platonic. It just won't be...'

'Stimulating? Passionate?'

She sought for a word. 'Stormy. Neither of us care for an excessive display of emotion.' Realising just how priggish that had sounded, she flushed and dipped her head, so that the long black hair fell forward, half curtaining her face.

Nick laughed harshly. 'Little Lord Fauntleroy can't have any good red blood in his veins if he's willing to settle for a tepid relationship like that. It seems as if your father was right when he—'

'Dad's not right. For once in his life he's prejudiced and—'

'Save your breath,' Nick broke in softly. 'It looks as if I'm going to have the opportunity to judge for myself.'

Kevin was advancing towards them over the grass, and for the first time she noticed that his shoulders were somewhat rounded and that he carried himself with a slight stoop.

Despite the warmth of the day, and the fact that it was a Saturday, he was conservatively dressed in a suit and tie.

Against Nick's smart but cool attire of casual cotton trousers and dark blue open-necked shirt, he looked overheated and overdressed. But, Raine was pleased to note, he was by far the most conventionally handsome of the two.

Determined to prove something, she exclaimed brightly, 'Darling...' Going to him, she flung her arms around his neck and stood on tiptoe to press her lips to his.

Kevin didn't actually *say*, Steady on, old thing, but he looked so uncomfortable that Nick had to turn his choke of laughter into a polite cough.

Raine glared at him.

Holding out a civil hand to the newcomer, he said blandly, 'I'm Dominic Marlowe—Raine's cousin.'

'Kevin Somersby. How do you do?' Pale eyes distinctly curious, Kevin shook the proffered hand, his grip moist but studiously firm.

Raine picked up her woolly and brushed it free of grass, then, slipping her hand through her fiancé's arm, asked, 'Shall we go up to the house?'

As though the suggestion had included him, Nick joined them, strolling along, sandwiching Raine between himself and Kevin, with a calm assurance that rattled her afresh.

Glancing from the slender black-haired girl by his side to the blond giant beyond her, Kevin remarked in his clear voice, with its upper-crust accent, 'I fail to see any family resemblance—though you mentioned you were cousins?'

'But not blood relatives,' Nick said shortly.

'Yet you have the same name?'

'My mother had been widowed and I was just a year old when she married Harry Marlowe. He adopted me.'

'I see.' Kevin nodded, before asking a shade condescendingly, 'What line of business are you in, Mr Marlowe?'

'The family call me Nick.'

'Then Nick it is.' The words were just a fraction too hearty.

With a thin smile, Nick went on, 'I take over small, near-bankrupt companies and make them into large, successful ones.'

Clearly disconcerted, Kevin adjusted his glasses and said awkwardly, 'That must be very satisfying.'

'It is, believe me.'

For no earthly reason, Raine shivered.

Calib had, as usual, made himself scarce when Kevin appeared. Now, to her annoyance, he emerged from a clump of purple Michaelmas daisies and attached himself to Nick with almost dog-like devotion.

Noticing the overt display of affection, Kevin collected himself and commented, 'The cat appears to know you very well.' When Nick said nothing, he continued a shade pompously, 'It seems a little strange that we've never run across each other before... In fact, I don't recall Lorraine ever mentioning you.'

'She's a funny girl,' Nick observed with a smiling, intimate sidelong glance at his cousin. 'Until today she'd never mentioned *you* to *me*.'

Kevin seemed unsure what to make of that. There was a rather awkward pause, during which Raine silently cursed Nick, before, either prompted by genuine interest or good manners, Kevin resumed the conversation again to ask, 'I take it you don't live in this part of the world... er...Nick?'

'I live in the States—in Boston, Massachusetts.'

'Ah... I wondered about the accent. I understand many *Americans* consider a Boston accent refined...'

When Nick failed to react to that piece of snobbery, Kevin went on, 'Are you one of the Boston Brahmins, by any chance?'

'Hardly,' Nick replied coolly. 'Though my mother's ancestors came over on the *Mayflower*.'

'What on earth is a Boston Brahmin?' Raine asked.

It was Nick who answered. 'It's a name coined by Oliver Wendell Holmes back in the nineteenth century to describe the ''aristocracy''—wealthy merchants of the city who were well-read, well-travelled and very conservative. They were usually descendants of the early Puritan settlers.'

As they left the walled garden and began to walk up the gentle slope of green lawns that led to the house, with its rosy brick herringbone-patterned walls and overhanging eaves, Kevin smoothed back his already smooth hair and pursued the matter. 'So, have you two known each other all your lives?'

Nick shook his head. 'We didn't get to know each other until...when would it be, Raine?'

She ground her teeth. 'I don't remember exactly.'

'Oh, I'm sure you do.' He caught and held her glance.

The gleam in his dark blue eyes brought a quick flush of betraying colour to her cheeks.

'About a year ago, I suppose.' Her tone was as offhand as she could make it.

'It's rather a romantic story,' Nick went on conversationally. 'Wouldn't you say so, honey?' Then, turning to the other man, he went on, 'You see, when—'

Afraid of that "honey", and of what he might be about to reveal, Raine interrupted jerkily, 'I'm sure Kevin won't want to be bored by all the family history.'

'Not at all,' Kevin said politely. Then to Nick, 'Do go on.'

Cocking an eyebrow at Raine, Nick suggested, 'Perhaps *you'd* like to carry on?'

Caught between the devil and the deep blue sea, she chose the latter, and, estimating the distance to the house, began at the part she didn't mind telling.

'Nick's—' she spoke the hated name with difficulty '—adoptive father and mine were twins. More than thirty years ago they quarrelled and lost touch. Then last autumn, quite unexpectedly, we heard from Uncle Harry. He had just been diagnosed as suffering from a terminal illness and he wanted to make up the quarrel while he could. Dad and I went over to Boston.'

Leading the way over the old crazy-paving into the house, Raine added, as though it didn't matter, 'And that's when Nick and I met for the first time.'

Crossing the hall, she opened the door into the long, wood-panelled, black-beamed lounge. A comfortably faded chintz-covered suite and some lovingly cared for antiques stood on the polished oak floorboards. Bowls of autumn flowers glowed in dark corners, and a huge jar of bronze chrysanthemums filled the stone fireplace.

Ralph glanced up from the detective story he was reading. In the past he'd always been too much of a workaholic to relax, but whiplash injuries sustained in a minor road accident that year had left him with pains in his back and chest, and he'd been warned to take it easy.

For once in his life, Raine was pleased to see, he seemed to be obeying his doctor's orders.

He took off his glasses, put down his book and smiled at the little group, revealing a gap between his two front teeth that gave him an endearingly boyish look.

He addressed his daughter. 'Martha has just been in to ask how many there'll be for dinner tonight.' His enquiring glance at Kevin, though civil, lacked warmth. 'So if you'd care to tell her?'

Her voice cool and composed now, Raine asked, 'Is Nick staying?'

Ralph's hazel eyes showed his annoyance. 'Of course he's staying.'

'Then there'll be just the two of you.' She moved closer to her fiancé. 'We have other plans for the evening—haven't we, darling?'

Her father frowned. 'Other plans?'

'When I've got changed we're going in to Lopsley. Kevin's taking me to Phasianidae.'

'What the deuce is that?' her father demanded irritably.

'A new restaurant that's just opened in Cheyne Walk.'

Ralph glanced helplessly at his nephew.

'So you'll have to forgive us for not joining you.' Raine gave Nick a disdainful little smile. 'I'm sure you and Dad can find plenty to talk about.'

'I'm sure we can,' he agreed smoothly. 'But it's *you* I need to talk to.'

Her face froze into a stiff mask. 'Anything you want to say to me will presumably keep until tomorrow.'

'Unfortunately it won't.' Turning, Nick clapped a hand on Kevin's shoulder. 'We've come up against something of a family problem that needs sorting out immediately. I know you'll understand, and I'm quite sure that in the circumstances you wouldn't want to...' He allowed the words to tail off.

'No…no, of course not.' Reacting to the hint of cool authority that lay beneath the friendly tone, Kevin was already backing away.

Alarm made Raine dig her toes in. 'I really don't see what's so urgent that it can't wait until the morning.'

Catching Nick's peremptory glance, Kevin said hastily, 'Don't worry, old thing. We can always go some other time. I'll cut along now and come over early tomorrow, if that's all right by you?'

Desperate to keep her fiancé as a buffer between herself and Nick, Raine appealed to her father. 'But Kevin will soon be part of the family. Surely he can stay?'

It was Nick who answered. 'He *can*, but…' You won't really want him to, the dark blue eyes warned her.

Brought up short, she hesitated.

As though he owned the place, Nick moved to shepherd Kevin out, adding in a jocular tone, 'Perhaps it's better not to know about the family skeletons until *after* you're married.'

In the doorway he glanced back, and Raine saw an odd look pass between him and Ralph before the latch clicked to behind him.

Fuming helplessly, a flush of colour lying along the wide cheekbones inherited from her mother, she turned to Ralph and asked in a choked voice, 'What's he doing here?'

'I sent for him.'

'Why didn't you *tell* me he was coming?'

'Because last time I told you he was coming you bolted.'

'I didn't want to see him,' she said defensively.

'Damn it, girl,' Ralph exploded, 'have you any idea how *furious* you made him? He hung around here for over a week—a week he really needed to be in Boston.

'You made him look a complete fool, and you ought to know he's not a man to tolerate that sort of treatment. Why hadn't you the decency to stay and listen to him?'

'I didn't want to hear anything he had to say. I still don't.'

Almost wearily, Ralph said, 'Well, you can't keep on avoiding him. He's here now, and you'll have to face him.'

CHAPTER THREE

RAINE shook her head, silently repudiating that statement. As far as she was concerned she didn't have to do anything of the kind. It had been her fixed intention never to see him again.

In spite of her father's pleas, and to her everlasting shame, she had even chickened out of going to her uncle's funeral because *he'd* be there.

It would be a relief when she was safely married, she thought fervently, while her stomach remained tied in a knot of tension. Though it would mean leaving her father and the home she loved, at least she wouldn't have to risk coming face to face with Nick out of the blue like this.

But it wasn't really out of the blue. Her father had asked him to come. Suddenly, without knowing why, she was scared stiff. 'What made you send for him?'

Looking uneasy, anything but comfortable, Ralph said, 'The doctor advises that I don't go back to the office for at least three months.' Involuntarily, his hand had gone up to touch his chest.

'Your heart...?' she whispered.

'There's nothing wrong with my heart. I'm as fit as a fiddle,' he said testily. 'But I...well, I'm not getting any younger, and I...'

'Oh, Dad...' She went down on her knees by his chair.

'Don't be a fool, girl.' He patted her hand. 'Now, get up, and believe me when I tell you that I'm not ill. I'd just like to take it easy for a while. That's where Nick comes in...'

'How do you mean?' But already a cold chill was raising the short hairs on the back of her neck and running down her spine.

'I mean he's going to take the reins temporarily.'

'But couldn't I do that?' she protested, rising to her feet.

Shaking his head, Ralph reminded her, 'You're getting married soon, and if Kevin doesn't want you to work...'

'Well, can't David Ferris cope? He's been with you for years and he's absolutely trustworthy...'

'David's got enough to do,' her father said shortly. 'And I want someone up front who isn't soft—someone with initiative and drive.'

'But how can Nick look after your business affairs without neglecting his own?'

Ralph answered in a roundabout way. 'He told me once that, having watched his father work himself into an early grave, the most important thing *he'd* learned was how to delegate.

'Under Finn Anderson, his right-hand man, he's built up an efficient team who are quite capable of carrying on in his absence.

'Added to that, his business interests are varied and worldwide—so he can keep an eye on everything just as well from England as he can from the States.

'I'm well aware that things haven't gone right between you...' he said gruffly.

And that had to be the understatement of the century, thought Raine.

'But he's doing us an enormous favour. So *try* to be pleasant to him,' Ralph finished firmly.

Raine gritted her teeth. When her father spoke to her in that tone of mild reproach it made her feel as though she were a child again, instead of a woman of twenty-four.

'I know you were intending to take next month off to organise the wedding,' Ralph went on, 'but if you could spare a day or two to go into the office with him...?'

'No! I...' Fighting down blind panic at the thought of

having to come into close contact with Nick on a daily basis, she managed more moderately, 'I'm sorry, Dad, but I won't have time.'

Hardening her heart against her father's disappointed face, she went on hurriedly, 'In fact, I won't *be* here. Because the wedding reception is being held in Mayfair, Lady Somersby has suggested that I stay with her in Manton Square until the final seating plan and all the last-minute details have been decided on...'

For the past two weeks Raine had been politely resisting the suggestion, but now it seemed the lesser of two evils.

'So when Kevin comes tomorrow, I intend to go back to town with him.'

'You're running away again,' Ralph accused her, a kind of anxious irritation in his hazel eyes.

'I'm doing nothing of the kind,' she denied. 'I—I *need* to be on the spot to help complete the arrangements and cope with any possible hitches...'

Some slight sound made them both look up.

Nick was standing there, his broad shoulders filling the doorway. Judging by his derisive expression, he'd overheard enough to put him in the picture.

When he spoke, his manner was as cool and hard as ice-clad marble. 'Before you make any further arrangement, we really should have that talk.'

Managing to sound distant and haughty, Raine informed him, 'I've just talked to Dad. It's kind of you to help him out, and I'm grateful, but...'

Nick's handsome eyes glinted as he warned, 'Don't patronise me, Raine.'

Flushing a little, despite herself, she ploughed on, 'But it doesn't involve me, and—'

'Don't be too sure about that. Though your father's put you partly in the picture, you'll understand much better when you've heard what I have to say.'

The eyes of the two men met.

'If you'll excuse me.' Ralph got to his feet. 'I'd better

let Martha know how many there are for dinner, or we won't be getting any.'

With calm effrontery, Nick said, 'I was intending to take Raine out for a meal, if that's all right with you?'

'Fine by me,' Ralph agreed genially.

For a moment she was speechless, then, as the door closed behind her father's tall, spare figure, she turned on Nick furiously. 'I wouldn't have dinner with you if you were the last man on earth.'

'Not a very original remark,' he taunted.

'Original or not, I mean it. I don't know how you've got the nerve to suggest such a thing after you've completely ruined the evening...'

'The evening's not over yet,' he pointed out, a strange note in his voice. Then, watching her involuntary shiver, he added in a bored tone, 'Now, do go and get ready, there's a good girl.'

'This late on a Saturday night you won't get in anywhere without a reservation.' She made no attempt to hide the triumph. 'We'll end up eating in the local snack-bar.'

He merely smiled. 'I've already booked a table for two at the Priest House.'

The Priest House, a beautiful old building dating from the fifteen-hundreds, was the most expensive and exclusive restaurant in the neighbourhood.

'How *dare* you do such a thing without even asking me?' she burst out. Then, realising that by losing her temper she was playing into his hands, she drew a deep breath and went on more calmly, 'I'm afraid you'll be eating alone. I'd rather starve than accept your invitation.'

Nick's face hardened. 'My dear Raine, you don't seem to understand... It isn't an invitation. It's an order.'

Furiously, she demanded, 'What makes you think you can give me orders?'

With a smile that showed the gleam of his white teeth but failed to reach his eyes, a smile that was a danger signal, he said with terrifying confidence, 'Because I hold the whip hand.'

She wanted to deny his assertion, to protest that he was joking, or mistaken, or mad, but, knowing the man, she was suddenly convinced that he was none of those things. That he somehow *did* hold the whip hand.

Feeling as though she'd been punched in the solar plexus, Raine stared up at him mutely, her clear green eyes startlingly beautiful.

'My, what big eyes you've got,' he murmured mockingly.

Finding her voice, she said through stiff lips, 'If you think I'm going to take orders from you just because you're helping Dad out…'

But it didn't need his silence to convince her that his autocratic statement was based on a great deal more than that. In exasperation, she cried, 'Well, if it isn't that, what *is* it?'

'I'll tell you after we've eaten. Now, suppose you go and get changed?' Though phrased as a suggestion it was undoubtedly an order. And he wanted her to know it.

As she turned blindly away he cautioned, 'Oh, and Raine, until you know exactly how things stand, it wouldn't be wise to worry your father.'

On legs that shook a little, she hurried up the dark-oak crimson-carpeted stairs to the pleasant, lattice-windowed room she'd had since childhood.

''It wouldn't be wise to worry your father…'' While she showered the quiet warning kept ricocheting around her mind, making her wonder if Nick knew something her father was keeping from her.

Well, it was no use getting worked up about it, Raine told herself firmly, but at the first opportunity she'd have a word with Dr Broadbent.

Hands unsteady, she pulled on a silky lilac dress with a matching jacket and, to counteract Nick's intimidating height, high-heeled sandals.

Too het up to bother with make-up, she pulled a comb through her smooth, glossy, below shoulder-length hair and picked up her bag; she was ready.

Quick as she'd been, Nick was waiting for her in the hall. He'd changed into a well-cut, lightweight suit and a pearl-grey tie, and his thick blond mane was parted on the left and neatly brushed.

Standing arrogantly at ease, head tilted a little, one hand thrust into his trouser pocket, he watched her come down the stairs, long-legged and elegant, her slender body moving gracefully.

'Full marks for speed...' he commented with satisfaction. Then, tilting her chin with a proprietorial hand, he studied her exquisitely boned face with its black winged brows and wide-spaced almond eyes, straight nose and generous mouth.

His gaze lingered on her mouth.

'Don't!' she said sharply.

'You have no lipstick to smudge...'

She froze into immobility and closed her eyes as his mouth moved closer and hovered. But the kiss never came. With delicate cruelty he nipped her full lower lip between his white teeth.

When her lids flew open, he said flatly, 'Even without make-up you're still the most beautiful woman I've ever seen.'

Badly shaken, she tried mockery. 'In a minute you'll be telling me Kevin's a lucky man.'

'That's a matter of opinion. Personally, I rate the willingness to trust a great deal higher than looks.'

The chilling put-down was delivered with a complete lack of emotion. Still it stung.

Jerking free, she retorted, 'Was I the only one who was expected to trust you? Or did you ask your fiancée to trust you too?'

His mouth thinned. 'I would have explained how things

were if you'd given me a chance, instead of running out on me.'

'Apart from admitting you were an unprincipled swine, how would you have "explained" seducing me while you were engaged to another woman?'

'Hardly *seducing* you,' he drawled. 'As I recall, you were more than willing.'

Her face flamed. Unable to deny the charge, she said tightly, 'But then I had no idea what you were really like.'

'And you didn't stop to find out. You weren't prepared to even *listen*, let alone trust me.'

The accusation was full of anger and contempt. In that instant she knew that if he had any feeling for her now, it was hatred.

Well, that made them equal, she thought bitterly.

He lifted broad shoulders in a shrug. 'However, that's all in the past. It's the future I'm concerned with, and what I want from you now doesn't include trust.'

'What *do* you want from me?'

'Nothing you haven't already given me.'

That sardonic statement made her blood run cold. 'If you think—'

'I think we'd better get going,' he broke in crisply, 'before we lose our table.'

With a compelling arm at her waist, he escorted her across the hall, pausing only to open the door to the living room and call pleasantly, 'We're just off.'

Ralph lifted an acknowledging hand. 'Enjoy yourselves.'

The sun had set, and the scented air was still and velvety. Bats were flittering in the gathering dusk as they made their way to the stable block.

Nick's rented silver BMW was standing on the gravel driveway. With ironic courtesy he opened the door and helped Raine in, before sliding in beside her and fastening his seat belt.

Staring straight ahead through the windscreen, she wished she'd had the courage to tell him to go to hell and refuse to come. But he had a kind of quiet forcefulness, an inborn air of command, that made him a difficult man to stand up to.

Oh, come off it! she told herself scathingly, all at once impatient with her own cowardice. It was more than that. She was scared stiff of him.

Scared of his anger—just one narrow-eyed look could make her feel as though he'd backed her into a corner with his hand against her throat—and even more scared of his overwhelming attraction. His lightest touch could send her senses reeling and make her body long for his.

'Fasten your seat belt,' he instructed, and, when she made no immediate move to obey, he leaned over to find the buckle and snap it into place. As he did so his hand accidentally brushed her breast.

With a strangled gasp, she flinched away.

All movement stilled, watching her half-averted face, he remarked reflectively, 'You used to like me to touch your breasts.'

When, her breath caught in her throat, she said nothing, he deliberately stroked his fingers over the soft curve, smiling when her nipple firmed betrayingly beneath his light touch. 'It seems you still do.'

'No! I...I hate you to touch me...'

But his insolent caress had made her heart start to race, and the blood pounding in her ears almost drowned out the desperate protest.

His expression mocking, he withdrew his hand. 'Later on I'll put that statement to the test.'

Those soft words sounded remarkably like a threat, and she shuddered as he started the car and, tyres crunching on the gravel, they moved away.

The Priest House lay just over Sley Bridge on the outskirts of Lopsley, and the ten-minute drive was made in silence. To Raine, with every nerve in her body painfully aware of the big, loose-limbed formidable man by her side, it seemed like hours.

In the deep blue dusk the lantern-lit black and white half-timbered building, with its thatched roof and twisted chimneys, seemed to belong to a fairytale.

Tubs of autumn flowers glowed as if they were fluorescent, and yellow lamplight spilled from doors and casements open to the balmy evening air.

Their candlelit table was by the window in one of a series of tiny rooms—little more than compartments—that led into each other. The only other table the room contained was empty and bore a reserved notice.

They were served with an excellent dry sherry—"compliments of mine host"—while they studied the leather-backed menu.

'What do you fancy?' Nick asked.

Raine, who had never felt less like eating, replied, 'I don't really know.' Conscious of the discreetly hovering waiter, she added, 'Perhaps you could order for us both?'

He did so with aplomb, recalling, it seemed, all her likes and dislikes.

As soon as the waiter had moved away she leaned forward, but before she could ask the question hovering on the tip of her tongue, Nick shook his head. 'We'll eat first and then talk.'

She bit her lip, hating his easy command of the situation, the way he could keep her on the rack.

For the look of the thing they might have made polite, general conversation, but, taking him at his word, she remained silent, staring fixedly out of the window. If the waiter thought they'd quarrelled, so what?

Both the food and the wine were first class, but Raine scarcely tasted either, eating little and drinking less. Only too aware of Nick's eyes on her face, his critical appraisal, she had to make a real effort of will not to look at him.

Not until the coffee had been served and they were alone, did he enquire coolly, 'Well, Raine?'

Her nerves skittered wildly. She took a deep, calming breath and lifted her chin. 'I'd like to know what kind of game you're playing.' Ignoring the mocking twist of his lips, she went on doggedly, 'So now you've had your fun, perhaps you'll—'

'Oh, the fun is still to come.' Cutting off her words with the skill of a surgeon wielding a knife, he allowed his eyes to drop briefly but meaningfully to the soft curves lovingly outlined by the crossover bodice of her dress.

Then, watching her face grow hot, he continued tauntingly, 'And I'm looking forward to it immensely. If there's one thing you can't be faulted on, it's the passionate way you respond.'

What he seemed to be implying she refused even to think about. Reminding herself that it was only a month to her wedding, she tried desperately to fill her mind with images of Kevin. But, like a hollow man, nothing of substance was there. Even his features remained vague, indistinct, making him seem no longer real.

As though he knew, Nick smiled a little, before going on, 'And as for what kind of game I'm playing... It's no game. I've never been more serious in my life. Nor more impatient. Already I've waited for what seems an age.'

Mouth desert-dry, she asked, 'Waited for what?'

He moved his head and the light made his midnight-blue eyes gleam silver. 'You.'

Her heart lurched sickeningly. Endeavouring to sound unconcerned, even slightly amused, as though she thought he was joking, she said, 'Bearing in mind that I'm getting married in a month, haven't you left it a little late?'

'Would it have made any difference if I'd come earlier?'

'No!' The answer was swift and uncompromising.

'I rather thought not. Last time I came over you ran and hid, like the little coward you are.'

Fighting back, she snapped, 'Call me a coward if you like, but tomorrow I'm going up to London and I intend to stay there until the wedding. So if you have anything to say, it had better be now.'

'I've plenty to say,' he announced grimly, 'and the first thing is, *you're not going anywhere.*'

'You can't stop me.' They were bold words, and she wished she felt as confident as she sounded.

'Don't bet on it.'

She tried to scoff. 'You'll be telling me next that I'm not getting married.'

'You're not getting married. At least, not to Kevin.'

A chill which had nothing to do with the night breeze that made the candle-flame flicker goose-fleshed her skin. 'What do you mean, "not to Kevin"?'

'I mean you're going to end your engagement and marry me.' He sounded so calm, so matter-of-fact, that his words took a moment or two to sink in fully.

'You must be out of your mind if you think—' Raine broke off and, grasping at her self-control, counted to ten. Then, as though she were talking to a not very bright child, she said carefully, 'Six months ago Kevin proposed to me, and I accepted.'

When Nick continued to look completely unmoved, she added cuttingly, 'I know an engagement means very little to *you*, but to me it's a solemn promise.'

'I'm afraid it's a promise you'll have to break.'

'As you broke yours?' Seeing a muscle jerk in his cheek as he clenched his teeth, she pressed home her advantage, deliberately needling him, though she knew it was dangerous. 'I gather you and Tina never did get married?'

Remembering with a strange pang how Tina's pale, pretty face had lit up every time she'd mentioned Nick, Raine pursued, 'I know she absolutely adored you, so let me guess... Someone told her what a two-timing swine you were? Or you got bored with her uncritical devotion and walked out on her?'

Nick's eyes darkened to obsidian and his beautiful mouth compressed. Stonily, he said, 'Wrong on all counts. No one told her anything, and I didn't walk out on her. We were married just before Christmas.'

Shock hit Raine with the force of a fist. Still reeling from the blow, she stammered, 'B-but if you're already married…'

'I'm a widower,' he informed her bleakly.

'*What*?' she breathed incredulously.

His face a tight mask of pain, he said, 'Tina died.'

'I'm sorry. I'm truly sorry. I had no idea…'

'Of course you had no idea. You wouldn't listen, wouldn't let me explain. But without being aware of the facts you're quite happy to make snide remarks and—'

'I've told you, I'm *sorry*,' she broke in desperately. 'I wouldn't have been such a bitch if I'd known…' Then she said shakily, 'Nick, won't you explain now?'

'No, I won't. You had your chance and threw it away. From now on you'll simply do what I tell you. *Everything* I tell you,' he added with emphasis.

Alarmed afresh, she insisted, 'But you can't be serious about me ending my engagement?'

'I'm deadly serious.'

'Please, Nick,' she found herself pleading, 'you don't understand. It's three months since we set a firm date for the wedding. Things have gone much too far…I—I couldn't possibly end it now.'

Coolly, he said, 'Then I'll have to make sure that Somersby does.'

'Oh? And how will you do that?' Words and tone challenged him.

'If necessary I'll tell him all about us—about what happened last fall.'

She might have expected it. 'Do you think that will make him ask for his ring back?'

Nick smiled grimly. 'Don't you?'

Oh, yes. She knew Kevin's view—or were they his mother's?—on "casual" or even premarital sex only too well. Though it had never been openly stated, he was expecting a virgin bride, and, feeling guilty at deceiving him, she had prayed he would never suspect the truth.

When, pearly teeth biting into her lower lip, she remained silent, Nick insisted, '*Don't you*, Raine?'

After a moment she said weakly, 'He loves me.'

'But not deeply. I believe he's too shallow and inhibited to have very strong feelings. It's more the idea of a "suitable" wife he's enamoured of. A beautiful, undemanding, obedient wife, who will give him children without too much physical or emotional involvement.'

That reading of Kevin's character and his reasons for marrying was close enough to Raine's own unadmitted assessment to make her cringe.

Yet that was the kind of calm, dispassionate marriage she'd been looking forward to, she reminded herself fiercely. She'd had enough of being torn apart by passion and pain...

But Nick was going on, 'To put it bluntly, your aristocratic fiancé is a cold fish, and, if I'm forced to let him know what a passionate lover you are, as well as shocking him, it will probably frighten him half to death. So perhaps it would be less traumatic all round to simply tell him that you've made a mistake?'

Slender hands clenched together, she whispered, 'I *can't*... I don't *want* to...'

'Well, one way or another I intend to see the engagement is broken.'

'Even if it is, I'll never marry you.'

With easy assurance, Nick insisted, 'Oh, I think you will.'

A cold fear spread through her and she shivered uncontrollably. Spotting the betraying movement, he smiled.

Somehow she fought the urge to jump up, to run and keep running. Clinging doggedly to some semblance of calm, she queried, 'Would you mind telling me why?'

'Because you love your father.'

'If you think I'm going to marry you just because Dad would like me to...'

'No, because *I* would like you to.'

'I don't *want* to marry you,' she cried. 'I detest you.'

'Our feelings for each other seem to be mutual,' he told her trenchantly. 'However, I still want you for my wife.'

In a choked voice she protested, 'I've no intention of taking Tina's place.'

'Don't worry, you won't.' His tone flayed her. 'Tina was very special.'

'Then why do you want to marry me? I don't understand *why*.'

But suddenly she understood all too well. Nick was still mourning his dead wife, and he only wanted *her*, Raine, as a sexual substitute.

The next moment he confirmed her unspoken conclusion by saying, 'Because I need you in my bed. Ever since you ran out on me I can't get you out of my mind.' Just for an instant bitterness and some other emotion, keenly felt, showed through. 'It's as though I'm under a spell, and the only way I can think of to break it is to marry you and sate myself with you until the enchantment wears off.'

When she flinched, he added tauntingly, 'And the fact that you hate me will only add spice to our relationship.'

Raine felt sick and churning inside. Their last encounter had stripped her of all self-respect and left her an emotional cripple. The kind of relationship he was talking about now would almost certainly destroy her.

And, hating his own reluctant enslavement, he wouldn't care a jot.

It took a moment or two to control the growing panic and realise she was being a fool. Though he could almost certainly wreck her engagement, there was no way he could make her marry him.

Relief was flowing in like a warm tide when she recalled his earlier words, "I hold the whip hand," and the warmth slowly turned to ice. He wasn't a man to make a statement like that without reason.

With a kind of terrified fascination, a feeling of fatalism, she could sense a fine mesh of steel closing round her and imagine her own futile struggles…

Reading her cornered expression, he smiled grimly and remarked, 'You seem to be getting the idea.'

Trying to mask her fear, Raine retorted, 'I'm getting tired of playing games. It's high time you told me exactly—' She broke off as a lively party of four came in and, laughing and joking, were shown to the other table in the room.

'I think a change of venue is called for,' Nick said quietly, and signalled for the bill. As soon as it was paid, he escorted her out to the silver BMW, a hand beneath her elbow.

His touch was anathema to her, but, symptomatic of her feeling of being hopelessly trapped, she made no attempt to pull free.

It was a beautiful night, moonlit and starry. A sedate little breeze stirred the trailing ivy and ruffled Raine's half-fringe then, getting more adventurous, sent a few puffs of grey wispy cloud drifting across the deep blue sky like smoke signals.

Having settled her in, Nick took off his jacket and tossed it onto the back seat before sliding in beside her.

Hedged about by a barbed wire silence, they had travelled some three or four miles towards home when, ignoring Raine's quick protest, Nick swung off the main road and onto a narrow winding lane.

Their lights making a bright tunnel through the autumn foliage, they followed the lane until the banks on either side flattened out and he drew the car onto the grass verge beneath a stand of glorious bronze and gold beech trees.

Switching off the headlights, he turned towards her. In the gloom she could make out the strong lines of his face, the gleam of his heavy-lidded eyes above prominent cheekbones, the squarish chin marked with a slight cleft, the austere yet sensual mouth…

'There's no need to look quite so scared.' His voice was soft and mocking.

'I'm not scared,' she lied. 'But I don't want to be here with you. I want to go home.'

He reached to unclip their safety belts. 'First we need a private talk.'

She lifted her chin. 'All right—talk! Tell me why you think you can force me to marry you.'

'Because I'm in a position to ruin your father.'

CHAPTER FOUR

THOUGH quietly spoken, the threat seemed so melodramatic, so theatrical, that she wanted to laugh.

A glance at Nick's face, with its bleak expression and set lips, told her there was nothing to laugh about.

She sat stock-still, unblinking, her breathing rigidly controlled, while her thoughts wheeled and galloped about like stampeding horses.

Could this threat to ruin her father be just an elaborate hoax to try and rattle her, to settle old scores?

Of course! It was the only explanation that made any sense. And she'd almost fallen for it! She gave a wry grimace at her own gullibility.

With an insight that seemed to allow him to know just what was going on in her head, he remarked, 'You think I'm joking?'

'Aren't you?' She permitted a smile to curve her lovely lips.

There was no answering smile, and in the gloom his eyes glittered coldly. 'I'll let you be the judge of that when I tell you if it wasn't for me your father's business would fold.'

Wanting to repudiate that statement, Raine began to shake her head.

'If you don't believe me, ask him. Though I'd rather you didn't.'

'I'll bet!'

'Not for the reason you think.'

Palms clammy with cold perspiration, she demanded, 'How much does he owe you?'

'Shall we say a great deal more than he could possibly raise?'

No, it *couldn't* be true! Desperately she fought back. 'I'm aware the slump hit his business hard, but if things had been *that* bad he would have told me.'

Nick shook his head. 'He's been trying to keep it from you—that's why I'd rather you didn't speak to him about it. Your father's no longer a young man, nor in the best of health, and—'

'Nor in the best of health…' All her fears suddenly resurfacing, she broke in urgently, 'Has Dad got a bad heart?'

Looking startled, Nick assured her, 'No, of course he hasn't.'

But somehow the denial was too quick, too positive.

'Please, Nick, tell me the truth,' she begged.

'That is the truth. Believe me, there's no need to worry on that score.'

It sounded genuine, but still she got the impression that he was uncomfortable, hiding something.

Watching her expressive face, he added, 'You can always ask his doctor.'

'I fully intend to.'

After a moment, when he said no more, she battened down her fears and returned to the main issue. 'So you're trying to tell me—'

'I'm not *trying* to tell you. I *am* telling you that I've put so much money into your father's business that to all intents and purposes I now own it.'

'I don't believe it,' she whispered. 'You're lying.'

When he didn't deign to answer the accusation, her body motionless, her brain icy cold, Raine stared down at her clenched hands while she thought back over the past year.

The property market had been badly hit by the recession, and there had been times when her father had looked distinctly anxious, but he'd always made light of their difficulties...

"As you know, we lost heavily when that big development project fell through," she remembered him saying. "But things have started to pick up. We'll soon be climbing out of the red quite nicely..."

It was clear now that he'd been trying to save her peace of mind, to protect her as he'd always protected her.

How thoughtless she'd been, how blindly selfish! She'd gaily taken his word and allowed him to shoulder the whole burden alone.

And just a short while ago when, working out the budget for the wedding, she'd queried the present state of their finances, after the briefest hesitation, he'd said heartily, "Fine, fine... If you're *sure* Kevin's the man for you, spend whatever you need. I'd like to do my only daughter proud.'

Oh, Dad! she cried silently. I'm sorry... I'm so sorry...

With a warm hand beneath her chin, Nick lifted her face and turned it towards him. 'Having had time to think about it, do you still believe I'm lying?'

'No,' she said with bitter certainty. 'I'm sure you've done exactly as you say...' Jerking free, she went on, 'Tell me something, this idea of forcing me to marry you, how long have you had it in mind?'

Smiling grimly, he suggested, 'You tell me.'

'Since Dad told you that Kevin and I had set the date for our wedding?'

'Spot on,' Nick admitted, adding coolly, 'I've no intention of allowing you to marry some bloodless civil servant. Even if I have to use strong-arm tactics, I want you for my wife...'

Then he demanded, with a touch of impatience, 'Well, Raine?'

She shook her head. 'Go ahead with your take-over plan if you want to. All you'll gain is another business.'

Seeing Nick frown, she went on with more confidence,

'I'm afraid you've rather misjudged things. Though I'd be very sorry to see Dad lose everything he's worked for, as you yourself pointed out he's no longer young—in fact, he's getting close to retiring age...'

'Retired people have to have enough money to pay their way.'

'Kevin's not a pauper.'

Nick laughed with what sounded like genuine amusement. 'Can you really see Somersby going out of his way to help pay his *ex*-fiancée's father's housekeeper?'

Raine gritted her teeth. 'Martha wouldn't leave; she's part of the family.'

'She still needs some kind of income.'

'If I don't get married, I can take care of that. I'll find another job and—'

'It would have to be a highly paid one.'

Reacting to his tone rather than his words, she demanded, 'Why do you say that?'

'Because you would need to find somewhere else to live. You see, as well as owning the company, I hold the deeds to White Ladies.'

Shock hit her, making her huddle in her seat, stunned and motionless.

When her brain cleared somewhat, all the fight knocked out of her by the surprise of her opponent's two-pronged strategy, she felt only a dull acceptance of the *fait accompli*.

Nick had said, "I hold the whip hand", and he wasn't a man to make that kind of statement without being sure of his ground.

'Well, Raine?'

It was the same mocking query. This time the answer had to be different. There was no way she could let Ralph, who had been both mother and father to her for the past ten years, lose the home he loved.

Turning to face the formidable man by her side, she tried for some kind of compromise—something not so binding as marriage. 'Suppose I agree to sleep with you whenever you want.'

Nick laughed harshly. 'If you think I'm going to be satisfied with creeping into your room each night as though we're having some clandestine affair, you're quite mistaken.'

'All right—I'll live with you openly.'

'Wouldn't that upset your father? Without being in the least narrow-minded, doesn't he expect his daughter to have what he might term "good old-fashioned standards"?'

Then, like a cobra striking, he asked, 'Wasn't that why you failed to tell him what happened a year ago?'

Glad of the gloom that helped to hide her burning face, Raine demanded thickly, 'How do you know I didn't tell him?'

'Because when you ran and hid when I came over, and it became clear that you were determined to have nothing more to do with me, I told him myself.'

'You *what*?' she spluttered.

'I told him myself,' Nick repeated flatly.

'Oh, how *could* you?' She was almost frantic. 'You had no right to tell him.'

Nick disagreed coolly. 'I was involved, and in the circumstances I thought it best.'

'I don't—'

He put a lean finger against her lips, stopping the angry words. 'It occurred to me that you might be pregnant, and desperate enough to do something foolish.'

'You mean have an abortion! I would *never* have done such a thing...'

'Well, I couldn't be sure of that, and, having commitments in Boston—'

'In the form of a fiancée,' she interrupted bitterly.

A tightening of his jaw muscles was the only sign that her words had struck home before he went on evenly, 'At that time, for both personal and business reasons, I couldn't stay in England indefinitely, so I wanted Ralph to know the score.'

Then, answering her unspoken question, Nick added gently, 'On the whole he took it very well. Afterwards we had a drink together and he told me about Beatrice...which explained a lot...'

Raine was startled. To the best of her knowledge her father had never talked about his much loved younger sister to anyone else. Beatrice had been sweet and beautiful, but wild. Amoral rather than immoral, she had died at nineteen from the effects of an illegal abortion.

Raine's eyes filled with tears. After all his care and concern to bring *her* up with good moral values, her father must have been terribly hurt and saddened. But his attitude towards her hadn't changed in the slightest. He had never blamed or reproached her, never given the faintest sign that he knew.

'So in the circumstances,' Nick was going on, 'I'm sure you wouldn't want to disappoint him a second time. In any case, as far as I'm concerned, it's marriage or nothing.'

She longed to scream, Nothing! Nothing! *Nothing*! Instead she said in an almost normal voice, 'And if I refuse to marry you?'

'Do you need to ask?'

She knew well enough that he could be completely ruthless when it came to getting what he wanted. And there was no doubt in her mind that he wanted *her*. Still she clutched at a straw. 'You might be bluffing.'

His voice was pure polished steel. 'I *might*—if you think you can afford to take that chance.'

She didn't. Somehow the very fact that he was refraining from putting on pressure made her all the more certain that he wasn't bluffing.

'What will you do if I marry you?'

A little smile curved his lips. 'Make slow, delectable love to you until—'

Heat scorching through her, she croaked, 'I mean about Dad.'

'As soon as he's my father-in-law the business and the house will be his again.'

'That's very generous,' she said slowly.

'I'm sure you'll be worth it,' he retorted sardonically.

Raine bit her lip. 'How long would you...?'

'Expect the marriage to last?' he queried when she faltered to a halt. 'Let's wait and see, shall we?'

'An open-ended sentence,' she said with sudden bitterness.

'If that's how you care to look at it.' There was anger in his voice.

'How else can I look at it? You don't really want me for a wife. You just want to use me as a...a sex-object, to rid yourself of an obsession.'

'Would you rather I said I loved you?'

'No!' she cried violently. 'I wouldn't believe you if you did. I'd sooner you were honest. At least I know where I stand.'

Then, because she couldn't stomach the thought of going back to Boston, to the home he must have shared with Tina, she said quietly, 'But America's so far away. And I...I'd hoped to be closer to Dad,' she finished desperately.

'Who said we'd be living in the States?'

She peered at his face, trying to read its expression in the half-light before saying hesitantly, 'I know you're expecting to be in England for a while, but...'

'If things go according to plan I was thinking of moving here permanently,' he said, and then, with a touch of impatience, 'And I'm quite happy to live at White Ladies, if that helps to make up your mind.'

It was an unexpected lightening of the load, but it didn't affect the main issue. She couldn't bear the thought of being married to a man who hated her, who only wanted to use her.

Suddenly she was filled with a searing despair—an old despair, yet much worse.

Once, believing he cared for her, she had found heaven in his arms. Now, heartsick and disillusioned, knowing he'd loved and married another woman, it would be hell.

But what choice had she?

Looking through the windscreen, watching with unseeing eyes a few papery beech leaves—colourless in the moonlight—float down and settle on the car bonnet, she said jerkily, 'I need time to think about it.'

'Very well. I'll give you until tomorrow morning. In the meantime…' Before she realised what he was about, he took her left hand and, sliding the solitaire from her finger, slipped it into his pocket.

'What are you doing?' she gasped.

'I don't like the idea of kissing you while you're wearing another man's ring.' His voice dropped to a husky murmur, 'And it seems a shame to waste such a romantic moon.'

'Don't touch me.' Her voice was suddenly shrill with panic. 'I hate you to touch me.'

'So you said earlier, but I beg leave to doubt it. *You* might not want my touch, but your body does. Do I have to prove it?'

No, he didn't have to prove anything. Already her heart was beating faster, and every nerve-ending was springing into life in anticipation.

But he sat quite still, making no move, and as the seconds ticked past the beat of her heart became so frantic it seemed to be in her throat, choking her.

Some instinct of self-preservation urged her to fling open the car door and run, but she felt spellbound, held in thrall. Neither the past nor the future had any reality; only the here and now mattered as she waited impatiently for his touch.

If she turned her head a little more she would feel his breath stir her fringe, and her own lips would be within inches of his brown throat…

Jerking back from the pit, her voice trembling, beyond her control, she demanded, 'Take me home.'

As if he'd read her seductive thoughts, rather than listened to her words, he brushed the black silky curtain of hair aside and bent to touch his mouth to the side of her neck.

'No! I mean it—no!' There was fright in her cry.

'Poor baby,' he mocked gently, 'you sound scared to death.' Before she guessed his intention he had shot the seat back, and, swivelling her body, he lifted her so that she was half lying across his knee, her hair cascading over his arm.

Trapped against his broad chest, feeling the solid bone and muscle through the thin fabric of his shirt, she begged in a hoarse little whisper, '*Please*, Nick!'

When his free hand cupped her chin and turned her face up to his, he saw the tears of fear and excitement that glittered in her eyes.

'There's no need to panic,' he said quizzically. 'Even *with* your co-operation I doubt if I could make love to you in the front seat of a car. The steering wheel gets in the way.

'In any case, I'm not as a rule in favour of what I believe is crudely termed "a quick bang". When I do make love to you I want the whole night before me—' his voice dropped to a husky murmur '—a comfortable bed and a long, slow seduction.'

He traced her lips with a sensual fingertip. 'At the moment I'm only planning to kiss you a little.'

'Don't...'

But the despairing protest was lost as he bent and remorselessly covered her mouth with his own.

She went rigid, lips clamped together, trying to resist...*trying*...

Lifting his head a little, he said deeply, 'Open your mouth and kiss me.'

The longing in his voice startled her, and, lips parted,

she was caught defenceless. This time he invaded her mouth, searching it so deeply that her whole being seemed to take fire.

Unable to quell the flames, she abandoned herself to the urgency of her own needs, to the relentless passion that left her shaking in his arms.

His lips caressed her temples, her closed eyes, the curve of her cheek. With little sucking, nibbling kisses he found the soft, velvety skin beneath her chin and jaw.

When his mouth touched the warm hollow at the base of her throat and his hand slid inside the crossover bodice of her dress she began to whimper—soft, involuntary little threads of sound.

The tips of his fingers stroked the curve of her breast, finding the sensitive nipple through the fine material of her bra, exploiting her weakness, her vulnerability, arousing her to fever-pitch.

She clutched at his hand, at the same time turning her flushed face into his chest. 'Don't… I can't bear it!'

'You want it and need it.'

'Not like this… Not at all…' She had hoped never again to feel the fierce needs that had betrayed her a year ago, leaving her ashamed and humiliated.

When Kevin had proposed to her she'd seen the chance to keep them safely under control, to channel her natural instincts into the kind of calm, placid relationship she could handle.

As though Nick knew her feelings *exactly*, he said quite gently, 'Don't be foolish, Raine. Just because your own sensuality scares you, you can't cut yourself off from human emotions, look at life through a mirror, like the Lady of Shalott…'

Oh, but she could—and she *would* have if Nick hadn't forced his way back into her life. To her it spelt peace, freedom from the kind of torment she was suffering now.

But, though lying next to his heart was torture, somehow

she had lost all power to pull away. Hopelessly, she whispered, 'I wish I was dead.'

'Look at me.' He put an imperative hand beneath her chin and turned her face to his. 'Are you really so desperate?'

Already regretting her words, she said, 'I've never wished such a thing before.'

'Answer me.' He spoke so harshly it shook her.

A kind of stubborn pride came to her aid. 'Don't worry,' she assured him almost jauntily, 'by tomorrow I'll have recovered the strength to fight on.'

She could have sworn he was both relieved and angry.

'Well, in that case I'd better make the most of tonight's weakness.' He found her soft mouth unerringly and ravaged it until every thought had flown and only sensation remained.

When he finally lifted his head, she was dazed and feverish and breathless.

Sounding abominably cool and self-satisfied, he said, 'As I promised, only a few kisses.' With a strong arm behind her shoulders, he helped her sit up and slide back into her own seat.

Deprived of the warmth of his body, she began to shiver, and, lifting a hand, rubbed her throbbing lips as though to erase the memory of his.

'That bad, was it?'

'I'd sooner kiss a toad,' she muttered.

Incredibly, he laughed, reaching out to stroke her cheek with a proprietorial hand. 'I've always understood you have to kiss a lot of toads before you find a prince.'

She sat stiffly, bitterly resentful, head up and slightly averted. How *could* he sound amused, entertained, when she felt so sick and churning? Jerkily she said, 'I'd like to go home.'

'Then home it is.'

He adjusted the seat, switched on the ignition, and, with

headlight beams swinging in a wide arc, lighting up the foliage, turned to go back the way they'd come.

As soon as the car was moving, Raine's tension snapped like an over-stretched rubber band. Drained and bone-weary, eyes closed, she slumped in her seat, unable either to think or feel, wanting only the blessed oblivion of sleep.

She was dozing as they drew to a halt outside the moon-lit stable block and she sat up with a start. Nick helped her out, and, leaving the car on the drive, began to escort her up to the house.

Dazed, still only half awake, she tripped, and he threw a strong arm around her. Though most times his strength scared her, just at that moment it was oddly comforting.

It was after twelve, and when he opened the iron-studded oak door, apart from the solemn ticking of the grandfather clock which stood on the lower landing of the stairs, the house was silent. Though darker inside than out, enough moonlight filtered in to make putting on a light unnecessary.

A hand at her waist, Nick followed her up the stairs, the carpet deadening the sound of their footsteps.

When they reached her room she would have gone straight in, but he stopped her, and, tilting her face up to his, kissed her lightly but firmly on the lips. 'Goodnight, Raine. Sleep well. I'll expect your answer in the morning.'

His last words should have precluded her from following that mocking order to "sleep well", but oddly enough they didn't. After cleaning her teeth like a zombie, she fell into bed and slept as though poleaxed.

Raine awakened slowly, reluctantly—unwilling, without knowing why, to face the newly laundered light of a sparkling Sunday morning.

She was lying blinking up at the black-beamed ceiling when memory opened the floodgates and she knew only too well.

How could she have been such a weak fool? After promising herself that it would never, *never* happen again, that she was mistress of her emotions, it was a cruel blow to find that she still couldn't resist him—that in spite of everything she had responded to his potent male magnetism with a helpless, self-annihilating passion.

But she seemed to have no defences against him. Though it shamed her to admit it, if he hadn't called a halt when he had, if he'd led her from the car and laid her down on the moonlit carpet of leaves beneath the beech trees, her traitorous body would have welcomed his rapturously.

And of course he knew that quite well.

She shuddered. No wonder he'd been so confident.

Oh, why, just when she'd got her life on an even keel, had Nick come back to destroy all her hard-won security, to put her on the rack again and demand the impossible?

But perhaps it *was* better to break her engagement. It really wouldn't be fair to Kevin to marry him, caring so little.

Though wasn't that the reason she'd agreed to marry him in the first place? Because she *didn't* care—because he had no power to hurt her as Nick had hurt her?

Poor Kevin! She felt profoundly ashamed.

His feelings might not run very deep, but he probably loved her as much as he was capable of loving any woman. So how, with less than a month to the wedding, and most of the arrangements made, could she bring herself to tell him she'd made a mistake?

Yet the alternative wouldn't bear thinking about. Nick was a fiend, a devil, and she didn't doubt for a second that, if he thought it necessary, he would be heartless enough to tell Kevin they'd been lovers.

But would he *really* ruin her father? The two men got on well together, each seeming to like and respect the other.

So what if it *was* just a bluff?

Once again she was unsure, uncertain.

When she'd suggested to Nick that he might be bluffing, he'd said, "I *might*—if you think you can afford to take that chance."

Only if she *did* take the chance and he *wasn't* bluffing, she could cause irreparable harm. It would be too late then to change her mind.

If Ralph were to suspect any hint of coercion she knew him well enough to be sure that he'd have nothing to do with it. He wouldn't want her to marry a man she hated for *his* sake.

So what was she to do?

After repeatedly weighing the odds, and thinking until her head ached, she was no nearer a decision. Getting out of bed, driven and restless, she headed for the bathroom.

When she'd showered and dressed in a fine skirt and top patterned in autumn colours, she twisted her glossy black hair into a knot on top of her small well-shaped head, put on a dab of make-up, then stood irresolute.

But she'd *have* to make up her mind. Nick would be waiting for an answer, and he wasn't a man to fool with. As he'd said, he held the whip hand. He owned the business and the house—everything that had once been hers and her father's. Probably even the clothes on her back...

Or did he? She only had his word for it!

What if the whole thing was a con—a lie from beginning to end? Suppose, after carefully setting the scene, he was relying on her *not* to question her father, knowing that if she did she would find out the truth...

Before the thought was fully formed she was out of her room and stumbling down the stairs. Throwing open the door to the sunny breakfast room, she was relieved to find her father there alone, reading the Sunday paper while he dawdled over a half-empty cup of coffee.

Looking mildly startled by the abruptness of her entrance, he peered at her over his horn-rimmed glasses. 'Something wrong?'

Hoping that her voice betrayed nothing of the anxiety

churning inside her, she said, 'No...no, of course not.' Then lamely, 'I just wondered if you were up.'

'Up? Certainly I'm up. It's after ten.' Tossing the paper aside and taking off his glasses, he reached for the cafetière and poured coffee for them both. 'You must have been late last night?'

'Yes... Yes, we were.' She went and sat beside him at the table.

'Did you have a pleasant evening?' The question was asked cautiously.

Biting her tongue, she managed, 'Very pleasant.'

'I'm glad you and Nick finally got together. To be honest, your unwillingness to listen to him has always worried me—and when Nick told me he'd like to talk to you in private...' He trailed off and then asked, even more cautiously, 'Did you reach any kind of...understanding?'

'About what?'

Disappointment showed briefly in Ralph's hazel eyes. After an appreciable hesitation, he said vaguely, 'Well, Nick had some plans he wanted to discuss with you...'

He'd had plans, all right! And when her father knew what they were he would see Nick in his true colours. But no, even then the devil was safeguarded. All he needed to say was that it had been a huge joke.

'That was why—'

'Dad,' Raine broke in, unable to contain her nervous excitement any longer, 'I'd like to ask you something—and please, *please* tell me the truth.'

'Ask away.' But though the tone was hearty, he looked anxious, ill at ease.

'How well has the business done in the past year?'

His eyes slid away from hers, and he busied himself putting his glasses in their case. 'Not too well, I'm afraid. But don't go worrying your head about that. Everything's fine now. Nick was willing to put money into the firm...'

Iron bands tightening around her chest, constricting her

breathing, Raine asked as casually as possible, 'How much money?'

Looking even more uncomfortable, Ralph admitted, 'Quite a lot, actually...'

So it hadn't been a bluff.

'That was one of the reasons I asked him to come over and take the reins while I'm at home.' He went on more jocularly, 'He has a vested interest, you see, and it's nice to keep things in the family.'

'Yes, you could say that.' Bowing to the inevitable, she lifted her chin and smiled brilliantly. 'Last night Nick asked me to marry him, and I've decided to accept.'

'Well, I'm delighted!' Ralph beamed his pleasure.

'I know it's all very sudden, and somehow...' She faltered and the smile faded. 'Somehow, at this late stage, I've got to tell Kevin our engagement was a mistake.'

Perhaps reading something of her very real distress in her face, Ralph patted her hand. 'It's better to realise it now than go ahead and find you're both unhappy.'

'You've never liked Kevin, have you?'

'It's nothing personal—just that I've never believed he was the man for you.'

'And you think Nick is?'

'Aren't I right? Though it's taken long enough for you to admit it. He's a fine man...'

Oh, Dad, if you only knew! she cried silently.

'And I'll be proud to have him for a son-in-law...'

She was surprised by the calm way he'd accepted what must surely have come as a bombshell—until she recalled the previous night's conversation and everything fell into place. Knowing, from Nick, that they'd been lovers a year ago, Ralph must have assumed that she'd carried a torch for her cousin all along.

'If only you'd been willing to listen to Nick before,' her father was going on, with an aggravating air of "I told you so", 'you could have saved yourself an awful lot of grief—'

'Dad,' she broke in urgently, 'did you know he's been married?' Just to say it was like twisting a knife in a wound.

'Of course I knew...'

Happening to glance through one of the diamond-leaded windows, Raine's attention was distracted by the sight of Nick—shadowed by Calib—and Kevin heading towards each other on a collision course.

Leaping to her feet, she headed across the hall and out of the front door.

In light trousers that hugged his lean hips and a white cotton-knit shirt, Nick looked lithe and fit, and very masculine.

Despite his casual clothes, there was an unmistakable air of command about him—a touch of cool arrogance in his manner that seemed to rile the younger man, who was very correctly attired in smart cavalry twill trousers, a woollen tie and a tweed sports jacket.

Raine arrived on the scene just in time to hear the two men exchange civil, but—on Kevin's side at least—hardly cordial greetings.

He turned at her approach. On his handsome, smoothly shaven face he wore a ruffled, distinctly belligerent look.

Knowing him, Raine guessed that, on thinking it over, he'd regretted his previous night's meekness, and had taken exception to being dispatched with such scant ceremony.

He came towards her and, apparently with the intention of re-establishing his rightful position as her fiancé, grasped her in his arms and kissed her firmly.

This totally unexpected and out-of-character behaviour took Raine by surprise, and it was a moment or two before she made any move to disengage herself.

Seeing that Nick's dark blue eyes held a dangerous glint, she said hastily, 'Kevin, I—I have to talk to you.' With a pleading glance at Nick, she added, '*Alone.*'

CHAPTER FIVE

SEIZING Kevin's arm, she hurried him towards the house. To her great relief the living room was empty. Drawing him inside, she closed the door behind them, and, waving him to a chair in front of the flower-filled fireplace, took a seat opposite.

Frowning a little, alerted by her feverish manner, Kevin asked, 'Is there something wrong?'

'No... Yes...' Then she said baldly, 'I've got to tell you I can't marry you.'

He looked at her, his expression registering no more shock or alarm than if she'd said, I don't like your tie.

'I can't marry you,' she repeated a shade wildly.

'Don't be silly, old thing,' he said in mild rebuke. 'Whatever's happened to upset you, we can soon sort it out.'

She shook her head. 'No, I...'

Kevin's good-looking face grew tense. 'It's something to do with your cousin, isn't it? I thought from the start that he spelled trouble.'

'It's nothing to do with Nick,' she lied. 'It's simply that I've realised our marriage would be a mistake.'

A look of relief replaced the tautness. 'Pre-wedding nerves,' Kevin pronounced judiciously. 'That's all it is. Mother warned me it might happen. A lot of brides have second thoughts just before the wedding...even my own sister had some doubts. In a day or so you'll be yourself again and—'

'These *aren't* pre-wedding nerves,' Raine broke in jerkily. 'I'm sorry, truly I am, but I can't marry you.'

'Is it...?' He took off his glasses, wiped the bridge of his nose with a spotless handkerchief and replaced them. 'I mean, are you worried about the...er...the physical side of things?'

'No, of course not,' Raine answered, and, recalling her abandoned response to Nick's lovemaking, went scarlet.

Looking embarrassed, Kevin persisted, 'You know you don't need to be, old thing.'

'It's nothing like that.' Seeing that he was about to interrupt, she hurried on, 'It's just that I know now our engagement was a mistake. We're not really suited and I wouldn't make you a good wife.'

Something of her seriousness began to penetrate. Disturbed now, but still unwilling to believe it, he shook his head. 'You don't really mean that. By tomorrow you'll—'

'I *do* mean it. I can't marry you.'

Looking as though he'd been kicked in the stomach, Kevin stared at her.

Miserably, she said, 'I'm only sorry it's taken me so long to realise it.'

'But all the invitations have been sent out...' His ears growing red and his pale grey eyes agitated, he pleaded, 'You *can't* change your mind now!'

Damning Nick to hell, she whispered, 'I'm sorry...'

Jumping to his feet, Kevin cried, 'But what will Mother say? Lorraine, please...'

'I'm sorry, truly I am,' she repeated helplessly.

His face flushing, he cried angrily, 'You can't do this to me! Being jilted now will make me a laughing stock in front of all my friends.'

'I don't want to hurt you,' she said wretchedly.

'If you mean that, you'll forget all this nonsense and go ahead with the wedding. Mother need never know.'

Though she'd dreaded the thought of telling him, knowing his usual phlegmatic approach, she'd never dreamt it would be this difficult.

'It's not nonsense,' she insisted wearily. 'I can't marry you.'

'*Why* can't you marry me?' he persisted, his eyes beginning to protrude. 'What have I ever done to be treated like this?'

'You haven't done anything. It's all my fault.'

'Then change your mind. Whatever the problem is, I'm sure we can sort it out...'

For what seemed an age they went over and over the same ground—Kevin pacing backwards and forwards, growing angrier and more desperate as he failed to move her, and, with a tenacity she hadn't realised he possessed, refusing to take no for an answer.

She was close to tears of misery and frustration when there was a peremptory rap and Nick stood in the doorway, the cat winding sinuously around his ankles.

His grim gaze skimmed over Raine assessingly, taking in every detail of her unhappiness, confusion, and just plain exhaustion. 'Having trouble, honey?'

Furious at the interruption, Kevin demanded, 'Can't you see we're in the middle of a private conversation?'

Calib darted into the room and sprang lightly onto the arm of Raine's chair, where he sat like a statue.

At the end of her tether, afraid of trouble flaring between the two men, she begged, 'Please, Nick, leave us alone.'

Ignoring her appeal, Nick strolled over and, legs a little apart, one hand thrust into his trouser pocket, faced the other man squarely.

Though Kevin was tall, Nick was taller, and by far the better built, well-muscled and broad-shouldered, with a pantherish grace of movement that matched Calib's.

Unable to stay sitting down, Raine got to her feet and hovered anxiously.

Taking no notice of her, Kevin glared at Nick, and, too

enraged to be cautious, said, 'As this is nothing to do with you, perhaps you'll get out of here and—'

'Sorry, old boy—' Nick mimicked Kevin's cut-glass accent '—but it has everything to do with me.'

'I don't believe you. Lorraine said—'

'She was probably trying to spare your feelings,' Nick cut in crisply. Then he added, 'You'd better have this back.' Withdrawing his hand from his pocket, he tossed a small, sparkling object towards the other man.

Catching it with a reflex action, Kevin stared down at the diamond solitaire lying in his palm.

Reaching for Raine's hand, Nick drew her to his side. 'Tell him, Raine.' It was an order.

Somehow she said it. 'I'm going to marry Nick.'

There was a stunned silence, then, still without a word, Kevin dropped the ring into his pocket and made for the door.

With a cat's contrariness, or a feline knowledge of how to add injury to insult, Calib jumped to the floor and, running between his legs, almost succeeded in tripping him up.

Showing the extent of his fury, Kevin aimed a savage kick at the animal, which luckily failed to land, before slamming the door violently.

Nick whistled softly. 'Temper!'

Reaction setting in, Raine sank back into the chair and covered her face with her hands. 'I must have hurt him dreadfully.'

With a grunt that expressed his scepticism, Nick asked, 'How many times did he mention the word love?'

Her silence was answer enough.

'Then it's just his pride that's suffering. Come on, now—' taking hold of her wrists, he drew her to her feet '—stop worrying about Somersby. It's me you're going to marry.'

Repulsed by what she saw as his callous indifference to

the other man's pain, she looked at him coldly. 'Only because I have no choice.'

'Perhaps if you were to try and forget that—'

'Forget it!' She laughed incredulously. 'I shall remember it every minute of every hour of every day. And every time I remember it I shall hate you just a bit more.'

Some emotion—anger? Anguish?—darkened his eyes until they looked almost black, but his voice was indifferent as he said, 'Hate me as much as you like, so long as you sleep in my bed and I can take you whenever I want you.'

Flinching at his cruelty, she knew that all she'd succeeding in doing was to spotlight a relationship which, though unendurable, would have to be endured.

She shuddered, and shuddered again.

They were to be married on the last day of October in the small picturesque church at Lopsley. It would be a very quiet ceremony, with only the wedding party, White Ladies' staff, and a few local people present.

Finn Anderson, Nick's good friend and colleague, was stopping off from a business trip to be best man, while Margo Fleming, an old schoolfriend of Raine's, was to be bridesmaid.

Raine had wanted her before, but, because of a slight limp—the legacy of a childhood riding accident—Margo had been vetoed by Lady Somersby as "quite unsuitable" to be the bride's attendant with Kevin's sister.

After several weeks of dissension, unwilling to antagonise Lady Somersby further, and following a discussion with Margo, who'd said cheerfully, 'What the hell?' Raine had reluctantly given in and settled for a single attendant.

Ralph had mentioned that bit of unkind discrimination, and Nick suggested to Raine, 'Ask Miss Fleming this time. If she's anything of a friend she won't hold what happened previously against you.'

'I've no need for a bridesmaid,' Raine demurred. 'I won't be wearing a long dress or carrying a bouquet...'

Nick's midnight-blue eyes pinned her.

'I thought just a suit...' she finished uncertainly.

'Sure you wouldn't prefer sackcloth and ashes?'

Cringing at his tone, she nevertheless persisted. 'If we're getting married at a register office...'

'Who said anything about a register office?'

'But you've been married before,' she blurted out.

'I'm not divorced. I'm widowed...'

Widowed. Poor Tina, Raine thought, but the bleakness of Nick's face made it impossible to ask what kind of accident had caused his wife to die so young.

'The marriage service says, "till death us do part", so I'm quite entitled to be married in the village church.'

'Were you married in church last time?' She had to ask.

'No,' he answered shortly.

'Then why do you want—?'

'Leaving my wants aside,' he broke in, 'it's *your* first marriage, and there are your father's feelings to be considered. If only for the look of the thing I intend to have a traditional wedding: organ music and flowers and a bride in a white dress and veil... Though perhaps ivory rather than *virginal white*,' he added sardonically, and watched her flush scarlet.

Lady Somersby had presumed she would wear a white dress, and, feeling unable to argue, Raine had weakly accepted her dictate.

This time, against any kind of fuss, and unwilling to make vows she knew it would be impossible to keep, Raine had hoped to have just a civil ceremony, but, as Nick proved to be adamant and Ralph was strongly opposed to the idea of a register office, she reluctantly agreed to a church wedding.

The weeks leading up to it were a nightmare. Following the advice that Nick had given her—"Don't attempt to explain, and don't apologise"—Raine got in touch with all the guests invited to the Mayfair wedding, most of whom were the Somersbys' friends, advised them it was off and returned the presents she and Kevin had already received.

She also sent a note to Kevin and his mother asking their forgiveness and accepting the blame for the shambles they'd been left with; she enclosed a substantial cheque—provided by Nick—to cover any outstanding bills.

In return, Lady Somersby wrote bitterly denouncing Raine as "completely immoral" for "playing around with her cousin behind Kevin's back" and stating that in *her* opinion her son had had a very lucky escape.

Recalling her behaviour in Nick's car, Raine was unable to evade the guilty knowledge that to some extent the criticism was deserved.

Apart from a few hiccups, the Indian summer still lingered, but a cheerful fire was lit in the living room when the evenings began to draw in, and, on reading Lady Somersby's letter, Nick scowled, and, muttering a short, sharp expletive beneath his breath, consigned it to the flames.

Since that dreadful Sunday morning when Kevin had stormed out, Raine had seen comparatively little of Nick. Apart from insisting on a joint trip into town the next day to choose an engagement ring—a wonderful antique emerald bought and worn "for Ralph's sake"—and to make a visit to the vicar, he appeared to be deliberately avoiding her.

When they did meet he treated her with a kind of courteous indifference, seldom touching her and never kissing her. Only when Ralph was present did he make any pretence of affection.

He frequently worked late, and most evenings, after a bite to eat, the two men sat round a low table and played chess.

When Ralph expressed concern about the amount of time the younger man was putting in at the office, Nick excused it on the grounds of ''wanting to get the hang of things'' before taking time off to honeymoon.

Unable to bear the thought, Raine strenuously resisted the idea of a honeymoon, until finally, in exasperation, Nick demanded, 'Do you *want* your father to suspect there's something wrong?'

Biting her lip, she admitted defeat. 'No, of course I don't.'

'So where do you fancy? France? Italy? Switzerland, perhaps?'

She shrugged, and returned sweetly, 'Why don't *you* decide, as it's you who's so eager to go?'

'I'd prefer *you* to choose.'

'I really don't mind, so long as it's not Paris.' Paris was where she and Kevin had been going.

Keeping a tight rein on his patience, Nick suggested, 'Somewhere further afield, maybe? Madeira? Barbados? The Seychelles?'

'I really don't mind,' she repeated stonily,

At that moment her father walked into the room, and, apparently sensing some tension in the air, asked mildly, 'Not interrupting anything, am I?'

'Not at all.' Nick put a warm hand on the nape of Raine's neck, and beneath her hair he moved his fingers in a light, massaging motion. 'I'm just trying to get my future wife to select a honeymoon destination.'

Trying not to shiver at his touch, she pinned a smile to her lips, and invited gaily, 'Why don't you surprise me?'

With a glint in his dark blue eyes, Nick agreed. 'If you don't come up with a preference soon, I might just do that.'

'That sounds almost like a threat,' Ralph observed. Then, chuckling, 'I should watch it, girl. Bognor Regis can be a bit chilly in November.'

Since she and Nick had ''got together'', as Ralph put it, her father seemed a different man—younger, happier, much more relaxed.

Dr Broadbent had confirmed that Ralph's blood pressure

had gone down and, while denying any serious heart problem, admitted that his patient was now in much better shape. Raine could only feel thankful.

With very mixed feelings, but knowing that she must be sensible, she'd also discussed the subject of birth control. The last thing she wanted was to have a child, when the marriage itself was almost certainly doomed to failure.

The vexed question of a honeymoon wasn't mentioned again, and as the day of the wedding drew nearer, she began to hope that Nick had changed his mind.

When the morning arrived and he'd still said nothing, she breathed a sigh of relief, confident now that he'd given up on the idea.

Against all odds the weather had held, and the day dawned clear and sunny, with just an autumnal nip in the air.

Carrying her bridesmaid's finery in an array of boxes, Margo, her auburn hair curling around her small flushed face, her round, forget-me-not-blue eyes alight with eagerness, arrived a little after breakfast.

'Finished eating?' she asked.

'I'm not particularly hungry.' For days now Raine's appetite had been non-existent.

'Come on, then. Let's get started.' Without more ado the bridesmaid hauled the bride off to get ready.

Margo had been in such high spirits when the girls had visited a boutique to buy their dresses and wedding accessories that, unable to tell her the truth, Raine had been forced to put on a show of happiness.

'I'm delighted that things have turned out this way,' Margo had admitted. 'As well as being genuinely nice, Nick's such a *gorgeous* hunk of man...and so darned *sexy*.'

Seeing Raine blush, she'd continued with the garrulous frankness of an old friend, 'I never could understand what you saw in Kevin. I admit he's good-looking, in a wishy-washy way, but he *has* to be the world's worst prig. And that mother of his! You must be relieved not to be getting *her* for a mother-in-law.'

'Yes—I am, rather. In fact the whole thing was a terrible mistake.'

'I suppose you accepted Kevin on the rebound, so to speak?' Margo had commented sagely. 'It's always been Nick, hasn't it? When you came back from the States last year, though you never talked about it, I could tell something pretty earth-shattering had happened...'

Allowing Margo to draw her own conclusions, Raine had smiled and said as little as possible.

In her bedroom now, pale and silent, unable even to smile, she stood while Margo, bubbling over with excitement, helped her into the wild silk wedding dress and secured the filmy veil to her simple coronet of flowers.

She wore no jewellery except the emerald ring which, on the other girl's advice, she had transferred to her right hand.

The sound of a car engine drew Margo over to the window. 'The bridegroom and best man are just leaving,' she reported. 'But don't *you* look. It's unlucky to see your intended until you get to church... My, aren't they a handsome pair? I understand that Mr Anderson's over from Boston... Did his wife come with him?'

'No, I don't think he's married.' Raine answered the real question.

Her forget-me-not-blue eyes eager, Margo asked, 'So when did he get here? Is he staying long?'

Finn Anderson, a slimly built, personable man with fine dark hair and brown eyes, had arrived the previous evening. His handclasp had been warm and friendly, and, though it was the first time they had met, his smile oddly familiar. Smiling back, Raine had found herself liking him on sight.

'He didn't get here until late last night,' she answered. 'And I think he's flying back to the States about lunchtime tomorrow.'

Margo sighed. 'Pity. Apart from your Nick, he's the most interesting male I've seen for a long time... Ah, well...'

Not until the check-list of "something old, something new, something borrowed and something blue" had been ticked off, and Raine was ready, her small bouquet of creamy hothouse rosebuds at hand, did Margo prepare to leave for the church herself. At the door she turned to say, 'Don't forget to put your veil down.'

When her bridesmaid had gone, Raine stared at herself in the cheval-glass. Glossy black hair loose around her shoulders, face petal-pale beneath the circlet of flowers and whispy half-fringe—a frightened stranger looked back at her.

The fact that Nick had remained so cool and distant had given her a kind of spurious confidence, and, though she had gone ahead with all the preparations for her wedding day, somehow the whole thing had seemed remote, unreal as a bad dream.

Now suddenly it was here and all too real.

Still staring into the mirror, she recalled Nick comparing her to Tennyson's ill-fated heroine, and quoted aloud, '"Out flew the web and floated wide; The mirror crack'd from side to side; 'The curse is come upon me!' cried The Lady of Shalott."'

There was a tap at the door and Ralph walked in, immaculately dressed in a pale grey suit with a white carnation in his buttonhole.

Taking her hands, he surveyed her, his eyes growing misty. 'Bless you...you've grown up to be the image of your mother, and just as beautiful.'

Without conscious volition, Raine murmured, '"He said, 'She has a lovely face; God in his mercy lend her grace...'"'

'What?' Ralph looked startled.

Pulling herself together, Raine said, 'Sorry... For some strange reason Tennyson sprang to mind.'

'And is *The Lady of Shalott* relevant?'

'Of course not.' She managed a smile. 'I think I must be nervous.'

'Nervous or not, it's time to go.' His face suddenly deadly serious, he suggested, 'Unless you want to change your mind?'

There was no turning back now. She shook her head.

As though still doubtful, he pressed, 'You *do* love Nick, don't you?'

Green eyes met hazel, and she drew a deep breath to lie, 'Yes, I love him.' But even as she said it she knew it for the truth. 'I've never stopped loving him.'

At last she admitted it. Though it wasn't that simple... Bitterness and hatred and a kind of helpless anger went hand in hand with that love, making the ambivalence of her own feelings shock and astound her.

Under his breath, Ralph muttered a fervent, 'Thank God.' Then, aloud, 'If you love him I'm sure everything will work out.'

Raine closed her eyes against the pain. Nick had admitted that he hated her, that all he wanted was to cure himself of an obsession, and, as she couldn't bear the thought of just being used, the chances of things working out were virtually non-existent.

Leaning forward, she reached to kiss her father's cheek before pulling down her fine veil and saying with fragile composure, 'I'm sure it will... And I'm glad you think I'm like Mother.'

The familiar church, old and beautiful with its soaring arches and stained-glass windows, was full of sunshine and flowers and Bach.

Martha, a sturdy, grey-haired woman, dressed to the nines in a fur-collared coat and a hat with a feather, and Mrs Rudge the cleaning lady, also attired in her best, occupied the front pew. The gardener and his wife and a handful of villagers were scattered around the church.

But the only thing Raine was conscious of was her bridegroom, looking heart-stoppingly handsome in a charcoal-grey suit with a white carnation in his buttonhole as he turned to watch her walk up the aisle on her father's arm.

As she approached he held out his hand and drew her to his side. His hard-boned face showed a mixture of triumph and satisfaction, and some other strong emotion that was more difficult to decipher.

The church was very quiet as the ceremony progressed and the vicar asked, 'Wilt thou have this woman to thy wedded wife...?'

Like someone in a dream she heard Nick respond in a firm voice, 'I will.'

'Wilt thou have this man...?'

I have no choice... I have to go through with it for Dad's sake, she wanted to cry. But lifting her chin, she answered clearly, 'I will.'

If only things were different...she thought. If only Nick cared for her and this was a proper marriage... But he didn't, and it wasn't, and how was she to survive?

When his ring was on her finger, he turned back her veil and kissed her. His lips were as coolly aloof as his expression.

Then, the register signed, they were out in the sunshine and a photographer had popped up from nowhere and was taking pictures of the bridal party as they made their way to the waiting cars.

Less than five minutes later they were drawing up on the cobbles outside Ye Olde Flying Horse Inn, the sixteenth-century black and white half-timbered staging post in Lopsley's market place.

Laughing and chattering, the small group were shown into a private room with black beams, a crimson carpet, lattice windows and dark wood-panelled walls, where an early buffet lunch was laid out ready and champagne was waiting on ice.

The groom set himself out to be urbane and sociable, while the bridesmaid, the best man and the bride's father got on like the proverbial house on fire. If the bride had to make an effort to talk, and her smiles were a little forced, no one seemed to notice.

Standing by her husband's side, finishing her second glass of champagne, she decided that perhaps the secret of survival was to learn how to cope with the present and ignore the future. If she didn't allow herself to think ahead or anticipate what the coming night would bring…

Shivering, feeling her skin goose-flesh, she accepted another glass of champagne and gulped some down.

She was starting to feel curiously lucid, light-headed, almost buoyant, when quite suddenly she saw that the real secret of survival was simple. All she needed to do was use her will-power.

Nick had coerced her into marrying him, but it didn't follow that she *had* to sleep with him. If she made it abundantly clear that she didn't want him, he wasn't the kind of man to force himself on an unwilling woman.

Not even his wife.

No doubt, after that testing time in his car, he was expecting an easy victory, a walk-over, but he'd soon get fed up and put an end to the farce if she resisted, fought him every step of the way and *meant* it… It might not be easy, but she *could* and *would* hold out against his magnetism…

'You're not eating.' His voice, close to her ear, broke into her thoughts.

'So?'

Her militant tone made his fair, well-marked brows draw together in a frown. 'So I'll get you something.'

She shook her head. 'I'm not hungry.'

He seemed about to remonstrate when Martha appeared and came over to them.

'You make a lovely bride.' The housekeeper smiled tremulously. 'No wonder your dad's proud of you.'

As Raine gave the elderly woman a one-armed hug Nick queried, 'Everything all right?'

'Right as ninepence,' Martha confirmed. 'And before I

forget, here's the key. I'd better give it to the one with pockets...'

A moment later Ralph had put a glass in his housekeeper's hand, and, an arm around her shoulders, was leading her across to the buffet to ply her with smoked salmon and caviare.

'More champagne?' The best man approached the bridal pair, wielding a bottle of Dom Perignon.

'I think not.' Nick answered for both of them, adding smoothly, 'We haven't much time.'

'Why haven't we much time?' Raine asked as Finn turned away to refill the bridesmaid's glass. Her words were very slightly slurred.

'Because we have to get started soon... Our honeymoon, remember?' His eyes challenged her.

'But I thought... I haven't packed...'

'Martha's done it for you. She slipped away straight after the service, and your case is now in the trunk of our waiting taxi.'

Forestalling any argument, he added, 'She also brought your going-away clothes, and there's a room off to the left where you can change.'

When Raine made no immediate move, he relieved her of the glass and, smiling wolfishly, offered, 'I'll come and give you a hand to get out of that dress.'

'No!' Her slightly tipsy confidence instantly fled. A desperate glance showed Margo with Finn, her auburn head and his dark one close together, deep in conversation. 'I can manage.'

'I doubt it,' Nick said. Disposing of their empty glasses, he collected his bride's bouquet and propelled her towards a low door set in the panelling. 'You'd have to be double-jointed to reach all those tiny buttons.'

Having switched on the light, he ducked his head and followed her into a small, windowless room with a refectory table and chairs and polished oak floorboards. Closing the door behind him, he turned the large ornate key in the lock.

'What are you doing?' Even in her own ears her voice sounded high and frightened.

'Making sure no one barges in while you're getting changed. Did you think I was about to throw you on the floor and ravish you?'

When she just stared at him, with huge scared eyes, he said with a touch of violence, 'Don't you know your very desperation tempts me to do just that?'

With quiet, dangerous intent he moved towards her.

Oh, no. She couldn't be put to the test this soon. Not when she was unprepared. Unable to help herself, she backed away until she was brought up short by the panelled wall.

He put a hand each side of her head, palms flat against the wood, trapping her there.

Midnight-blue eyes caught and held green. 'Well, my sweet, *reluctant* bride?'

His lean, attractive face was too close, his beautiful mouth only inches from hers. Her heart began to beat with suffocating speed and heat engulfed her, her will *wanting* to deny but her body craving what he threatened.

Seeing his eyes darken with conscious and dangerous comprehension, she was beset by fright. If he once made love to her she would go up like ignited straw, all hope of resistance at an end. Then he would own her body and soul, and she'd be lost.

Somehow she found her voice and remarked carefully, deliberately, 'I thought as a rule you weren't in favour of "a quick bang".'

His almost imperceptible blink told her that she'd startled him, but his voice was smooth as velvet when he said, 'I could make an exception.'

'I'd rather you didn't.' She tried to sound blasé. 'You promised me a comfortable bed and...' Recalling exactly what he'd said, she faltered to a halt.

What could have been a gleam of amused admiration appeared in his eyes, before he finished for her, 'A long, slow seduction… Very well. If that's how you want it.'

The next second he had stepped back and was ordering briskly, 'Turn around.'

Removing the circlet of flowers with its cobwebby veil, he tossed it onto the table and, brushing her hair aside, with deft fingers unfastened the long row of tiny covered buttons. Then, sliding the heavy, rustling material from her shoulders, he allowed the lined dress to fall in stiff swirls around her silk-clad ankles.

As she stood in her dainty bra and briefs, his hands still resting on her upper arms, he bent and touched his mouth to her spine, his tongue-tip registering every slight bump and hollow between her shoulderblades and nape.

The sensation was almost unbearably erotic, and she shivered.

Drawing her back against him, he cupped her small, beautifully shaped breasts in his palms and, running his thumbs lightly over the lace, nuzzled his face against the side of her neck.

She made a small choked sound of protest.

While one hand held her prisoner the other slid up her slender throat to grip her chin and turn her face towards his. It was a lean, strong hand, long and elegant, beautifully modelled—a hand that knew how to be incredibly tender and passionate as well as ruthless.

Feeling a surge of desire, she closed her eyes, afraid of what he might read in them, while she waited helplessly for his kiss.

He looked down at her intently, studying the winged brows and long sweep of black lashes, the pale curve of her cheek against his dark-suited shoulder.

'My poor sacrificial lamb,' he murmured mockingly.

And then she was free, staggering a little with the suddenness of it, until he put out a steadying hand and helped her step out of the crisp folds of ivory silk.

The small case containing her going-away things had been placed on a chair. While Nick picked up her dress and wedding shoes Raine hastily pulled on a slip and a mint-green suit in fine wool with a cream blouse. Brown leather court shoes and her shoulder-bag completed the ensemble.

Having discarded his buttonhole, he asked briskly, 'Ready?'

At home she might have been able to cope, but now, faced with a honeymoon trip she dreaded... 'Where...?' Her voice cracked, and, moistening dry lips, she tried again. 'Where are we going?'

'To the airport.'

'And then where?'

'Boston.'

After the meeting with Tina had opened her eyes and made her realise what an abject fool she'd been, the place had come to hold such bitter memories that she'd hoped never to see it again.

With his almost uncanny insight as far as she was concerned Nick must have been aware of that, yet he still planned to take her there.

Anger boiling up, guessing that he'd chosen Boston deliberately to pay her back for her previous lack of co-operation, she rode the blow—perhaps she'd half expected it—and, gritting her teeth, informed him, 'I haven't got my passport.' Then, with a kind of desperate hope, she added, 'I'm not even sure where it is.'

Imperturbably, he informed her, 'I have it.'

Unlocking the door, he took her hand and taunted her. 'All you need to do is pick up your bouquet and present a picture of a radiantly happy bride.'

CHAPTER SIX

TO HER eternal credit, she did just that.

As soon as she had kissed her father, and Nick had shaken his hand, they made their farewells, and, amidst a shower of rice and rose petals, crossed the cobbles to the waiting taxi.

Raine paused briefly to toss her bouquet for Margo to catch, then Nick helped her into the back of the cab and they drove off, smiling and waving to the little group standing in the October sunshine until they were out of sight.

As soon as the need for pretence was gone, the cloak of happiness dropped away, and she sat stiff and silent, looking straight ahead, knowing what she had to face.

What made it so much worse was her unwilling attraction—she would no longer call it *love*, even to herself—to a man who neither liked nor respected her.

Realising that he'd felt nothing for her but lust, she had emerged from their first encounter feeling shamed and degraded. So how was she to survive a marriage founded on such a basis? It would be torture.

But if you walked into a torture chamber and agreed to be tortured, you could hardly complain about the pain.

Reaching across, Nick took her hand. When she tried to pull it away he merely tightened his grip. 'Listen to me, Raine. We're man and wife now, for better or for worse, so why not try to make it better?'

'You must be joking!' she cried fiercely. 'It's like asking

an innocent person who's been put on the rack to make the best of it, not to mind what torment it is...'

Almost wearily, he said, 'It doesn't have to be like that. You know as well as I do that we could be happy together. We enjoy each other's company, we share many of the same tastes and sexually we're compatible, to say the very least...'

Going hot and cold by turns, she scarcely even listened; only his last few words penetrated her misery and pricked her. If he thought he could turn her into some kind of sexual puppet where her will-power counted for nothing, he was mistaken...

'As for the rest, all we need is some kind of compromise—a willingness on both sides to live together amicably.' He squeezed the hand he was holding and coaxed, 'Why don't we call a truce? We can't go on making each other's lives a misery...'

When he looked at her with that almost irresistible appeal in his midnight-blue eyes she felt her angry resolve crumbling. She *wanted* to agree, *wanted* to banish the misery and find some kind of happiness.

But what happiness could she possibly find with a man who was arrogant and callous and quite determined to use her?

And why *should* she make it easy for him?

'Can't we?' Snatching her hand free, she spurned the olive branch.

He sighed. 'If you'd only stop fighting and look at things sensibly—'

'By "sensibly" you mean become a willing plaything until you decide you've had enough? No, thanks, I'd prefer to fight!'

His face hardened into stone. 'Then I'll just have to make sure that *I* win.'

The battle lines were drawn.

Their plane to Boston took off on time, and Raine, headachy from too much champagne and the accumulated tensions of the day, was thankful to leave the hubbub of the airport behind.

After the confrontation in the taxi, Nick had gone back to treating her with a polite aloofness, which, while oddly chilling, now left her free to pretend an avid interest in the paperback he'd bought her at Gatwick.

The flight proved to be smooth and uneventful. But, though Raine had been sleeping badly of late, with so much on her mind she was unable to rest—nor, despite Nick's frown, was she able to eat the meal she was served with.

The international airport stood on a peninsula facing the city, and as they circled to land she could see the bridges spanning the Charles River and the lights of Boston spread out below them like a bejewelled carpet.

When all the necessary formalities had been completed, Nick secured a taxi for their half-hour journey and helped Raine in.

As he took his seat beside her his thigh brushed hers, and involuntarily she moved further away. In the glow of the courtesy light she saw his jaw tighten, but he said nothing as he closed the door.

On her original visit to history-steeped, leafy Boston Raine had fallen head over heels in love with the place. Now, seeing it again, she felt she could recapture her earlier feeling of delight if only she could divorce it from the unhappy memories.

But that seemed to be impossible.

As the taxi drew up in Mecklenburg Place the door of number eight opened and yellow light spilled down the steps. It was like a re-run of the previous time, and just for an eerie instant Raine expected her uncle to appear.

But it was Mrs Epsling—a neatly dressed middle-aged woman with a pleasant face and soft brown hair—who came out to meet them.

The housekeeper greeted Raine with a friendly smile

and, while Nick paid the taxi driver and dealt with the luggage, ushered her up the steps and into the hall.

'It's nice to see you again, Miss Marlowe... I'm sorry—*Mrs* Marlowe...'

'It's nice to be back,' Raine lied.

'We were all delighted to hear the news of the wedding, and on behalf of the staff I'd like to give you our best wishes for the future.'

'Thank you.'

'Did you have a good flight?' she asked, then added with concern, 'You look absolutely worn out.'

Head splitting, limbs aching, Raine admitted, 'I am a bit tired.'

'If you'd like to go straight upstairs...?'

'Yes, I would.'

'Then I'll bring you a bite to eat on a tray.'

'Please don't bother. I'm not a bit hungry. I just want to get to bed.'

'I expect it's the time difference after the excitement of the day,' Mrs Espling said practically as she led the way up the graceful staircase.

Momentarily caught in a time-warp, Raine turned towards the room she'd used previously, but the housekeeper touched her arm and, opening a door to the left, showed her into the master bedroom. 'If there's anything you want, just ring.'

'Thank you, you're very kind.' But all Raine wanted was to lie down and sleep until she felt more able to cope.

As she glanced around the cream and gold elegantly furnished room, with its Regency striped wallpaper and elaborate cornices, a thin, fair-haired young man she recognised as Mrs Espling's son carried in her suitcase and placed it on a carved chest at the foot of the bed.

'Mr Marlowe said to give you this.' He handed her the key to the case.

'Thank you.' She summoned up a smile.

A quiet, efficient youth of few words, he gave her a respectful nod and departed.

When the door had clicked to she stood staring at the king-sized bed she would soon be expected to share with Nick.

A bed he must have shared with Tina.

Now that it was too late she wished with all her heart that she *had* chosen a honeymoon destination—as far from Boston as it was possible to get.

A shudder running through her, she unfastened her case. Ignoring the ivory satin nightgown and negligee that Martha had thoughtfully placed on top, alongside her toilet bag, Raine rummaged until she found a cotton nightdress and her old fleecy dressing-gown.

Off to the left was a cream-tiled luxuriously fitted *en suite* bathroom. Having showered and cleaned her teeth there with a kind of fierce concentration, she returned to the bedroom, switched off the light, climbed into bed and, closing her eyes, lay shivering, trying not to think of what lay ahead.

Perhaps if she was asleep when he came… Though it was a forlorn hope, she clung to it.

But, tired as she was, sleep stubbornly refused to come, and tense, on edge, she waited, listening anxiously for the sound of Nick's footsteps.

When he came, it was quietly—only the slight click of the latch warning her of his approach. Then she heard the door close softly and the brush of his light tread across the carpet.

Though she kept her eyes closed tightly and tried to breathe with the shallow evenness of sleep, she was aware that he had switched on the bedside lamp and was standing looking down at her.

Stooping until his lips almost brushed her ear, he whispered, 'I know you're not asleep, so you may as well stop pretending… Unless you're waiting for me to treat you like Sleeping Beauty?'

Her eyelids flew open, and he laughed softly.

He had discarded his jacket and tie and was in his shirt-sleeves. His thick fair hair slightly rumpled, his jaw roughened by the beginnings of a golden stubble, he looked devastatingly attractive and charismatic.

'Head aching?' he queried, studying her pain-shadowed eyes, her look of white-faced exhaustion.

'Yes,' she admitted hesitantly, wondering if he was going to jeer, to tell her tauntingly that it was too soon for the classic excuse.

Instead, he ordered briskly, 'Then sit up.'

When, hitching up the pillows, she obeyed, he settled himself on the edge of the bed and handed her a mug of hot milk well laced with brandy.

'I *hate* hot milk,' she objected.

Ignoring her surliness, he gave her a couple of round white tablets. 'Take these. They'll cure your headache and help you to get to sleep quickly.'

Seeing the surprise she was unable to hide, he queried sardonically, 'Unless you *want* to consummate our marriage tonight?'

She shook her head.

Watching her hastily swallow the tablets and begin to gulp the milk, he smiled derisively. 'No, I rather thought not. And as you obviously aren't in any condition to fight...'

'I wonder you don't take advantage of that. It makes me an easy prey.' The rash words were out before she could prevent them.

For a moment he looked furious, but his voice was quite level as he said, 'I can't raise much enthusiasm when it comes to "easy prey". I'd like to have a willing, or preferably *eager* partner, but, failing that, I'll settle for a good battle.'

Suddenly she recalled the little scene on the way to Gatwick when, refusing his offer of a truce, she'd thrown down the gauntlet, declaring that she'd prefer to fight.

And, being a man who clearly enjoyed a challenge, he'd picked it up, telling her, 'Then I'll have to make sure that *I* win.'

She knew him to be tough, with a many-layered hardness, yet he was also haughty and arrogant. He would want his victory to be a grand and sweeping one—a conquest he could gloat over.

Having realised she was too shattered to put up much of a fight, his pride insisted that he leave her alone.

When he'd waited so long?

But one of the most nerve-racking things about him was his self-control, his ability to wait… Another was his penchant for doing the unexpected.

A reprieve was what she'd wanted and hoped for, but, having been granted one, instead of being wholeheartedly relieved she found his forbearance strangely unsettling. It seemed to give him some subtle advantage.

Taking the empty mug from her hand, he put it on the bedside cabinet. 'Perhaps you would rather I made love to you tonight, so tomorrow you can claim you were too tired to resist?'

Shocked by the way he could read even her subconscious thoughts, she flared, 'I don't want you to make love to me *ever*. Especially in *this* bed!' she added distractedly.

'Don't you find it comfortable?' His words mocked her.

'It's nothing to do with comfort. I just can't bear the thought that—' She broke off, unable to mention his dead wife.

'That I shared it with Tina? Well, you can set your mind at rest on that score. No one else has ever slept in this bed with me.'

The relief was so great that Raine's green eyes filled with a sudden, unexpected rush of tears. She sat quite still, trying hard not to blink, but in spite of her efforts two teardrops escaped and trickled slowly down her cheeks.

His face softening, Nick leaned forward, and with a gesture that held something of tenderness he used his thumbs to brush them away.

She caught her breath at this intimate little action, and for some reason—perhaps because she was still overwrought, perhaps because just for a fleeting moment she saw how things *might* have been—she wanted to cry her eyes out.

'Come on, now, there's no call for tears.' He put his arms round her and cradled her close, almost as though he *cared.*

For a few seconds she abandoned herself to the delight of being held against his heart, before pride reminded her of the true situation and, struggling hard for composure, she pulled away, sniffing.

Having rearranged the pillows, he settled her down as though she were a child, and, brushing a strand of black silky hair away from her damp cheek, threatened softly, 'If you're not asleep by the time I've showered, I might be tempted to change my mind and make love to you after all.'

When Raine awoke it was to immediate recollection; her brain was instantly alert, warning her that she was sharing a bed with Nick.

A cautious peep confirmed that she was alone in the big bed, though the impression of his head on the neighbouring pillow made it plain that he had slept beside her.

The blue velvet curtains had been drawn back, and she could see calm morning sun slanting through the tall trees in the square, spotlighting the glorious autumn colours and turning the semi-transparent leaves to flame.

Glancing at the small gold watch on her wrist, and adjusting the time difference, she saw that she'd nearly slept the clock round.

The long rest had refreshed her. Her headache gone, she felt almost herself again—and ravenously hungry.

As though the thought had conjured it up, the door

opened and Nick came in carrying a breakfast tray. Freshly showered and shaved, dressed in casual trousers and a black polo-necked sweater, he looked fit and virile and incredibly handsome.

Settling the tray across her knee, he asked, 'Feeling better?'

Though her heart had begun to race, she answered with cool politeness, 'Fine now, thank you,' and wondered why he was waiting on her.

'Hungry, I hope?'

'Yes.' She avoided meeting his eyes.

'That's good. Otherwise I was going to have to force-feed you.'

In spite of the smile that accompanied his words, she felt certain that he wasn't joking.

Lifting the cover from a dish of fluffy scrambled eggs with thin strips of crispy bacon, accompanied by a pile of palm-sized buckwheat pancakes and a small brown jug of maple syrup, he invited, 'Make a start.'

Apart from twin coffee-cups, the tray was set for one. Uncomfortable at the thought of him just sitting there watching her, she asked, 'Aren't you eating?'

'I had breakfast an hour ago. But I'll have some coffee.' He filled two cups with the fragrant brew, and, carrying his over to the window, stood, his broad back to the room, looking out across the square.

Grateful for his tact, Raine tucked in with a will. She had eaten most of the eggs and bacon and, not caring to mix sweet and savoury in the way most Americans did, was finishing off with a syrup-doused pancake before he turned.

Replete, mouth and fingers delectably sticky, she sighed. 'Mmm...that was delicious.'

He put the tray on an occasional table and came to sit on the edge of the bed. Suddenly he was too big, too male, too nerve-rackingly close.

Lifting her hand, his eyes holding hers, he separated her

index finger and took it between his white teeth for a moment, before sliding it into his mouth and sucking the sweetness from it with leisurely enjoyment.

She gasped, and her eyes widened.

Her thumb and middle finger got the same erotic treatment, while her stomach clenched and her nipples tingled.

Seeing his gaze drop to her mouth, she swallowed convulsively. Leaning forward, he licked along her bottom lip with delicate little flicks of his tongue that made her start to tremble.

Then his mouth was brushing hers, teasing, tantalising, sucking and nibbling at the sweet velvety softness of her lips.

But when they parted for him he said softly, 'I'm giving you fair warning. If I kiss you once I shall come back to bed and spend the day making love to you… Do you *want* me to kiss you?'

Though her whole being cried, Yes, oh, yes, she managed to bite back the words. Why was he giving her the option? If he'd just carried on she would almost certainly have been putty in his hands.

Though he'd said how much he wanted her, and that he intended to win the battle, he seemed to be bending over backwards to avoid any accusation of coercion.

But if he could force her to admit that *she* wanted *him*, then surely the battle was won? And she *did* want him. So much so that if he once made love to her she would be lost. A plaything he could use and discard at will. A toy he could break.

So the last thing she must do was admit it.

'Well, Raine?'

'No!' she cried hoarsely.

He drew back, and, his voice cool, almost casual, remarked, 'Then we shall have to find some other way to fill the day. What would you like to do?'

'I'd like to walk out of here and never have to set eyes on you again. Failing that, I really don't care.'

Controlling his irritation, he said, 'You'll need some more clothes—I told Martha to pack only the essentials—so I suggest we go shopping, and you can reacquaint yourself with Boston.'

Her earlier resentment at the fact that he'd deliberately chosen a place he *must* know she dreaded revisiting flared up. 'I'd rather not,' she said shortly, and looked away.

Studying her half-averted face, he remarked, 'I take it you don't care overmuch for your honeymoon destination?'

Reacting to his mocking tone, she asked sweetly, 'What on earth makes you think that?'

'You don't exactly look delirious with joy at the prospect of seeing it again.'

'Did you imagine I would be?' Her voice was brittle.

Nick smiled bleakly and, probing her reluctance, remarked, 'As far as I recall, the only place you actually vetoed was Paris. The first time you came to Boston you enjoyed it...'

'But this time it was meant to be a punishment,' she said resentfully.

'It was meant to be in the nature of a breathing-space—a day or two alone to—'

'The last thing I want is to be alone with you,' she broke in coldly.

His face hardened. 'I thought it would give you a chance to come to terms with the situation.'

She laughed harshly. 'You expect me to come to terms with the fact that I've been forced to marry a man I loathe and detest?'

Holding onto his patience, ignoring the deliberate provocation, he told her, 'We don't need to stay in Boston. If you want to we can leave today...'

Soft lips pressed together, she refused to answer.

Though plainly exasperated by her silence, he said reasonably, 'There's no point in making things worse. All I'm asking is a little co-operation in order to make our honeymoon as pleasant as possible. If you'll just tell me where you'd like to go...'

When once again, her expression sardonic, she failed to respond, he took her shoulders and shook her slightly. 'Look, Raine, I don't want you to hate me any more than you already do, so if—'

Sensing that he meant it, she tried deliberately to wound him. 'That would be impossible.'

With a kind of bitter self-mockery, he said, 'Then what have I got to lose?'

'Not a thing.' She twisted the knife. 'And it doesn't matter *where* we go for our so-called honeymoon. As far as I'm concerned, one hell is as good as another.'

For a moment his fingers tightened painfully, then, as though he didn't trust himself not to hurt her, he let her go and stood up.

'Very well.' He was coldly, quietly furious. 'If you're determined to go on fighting, and you *want* it to be hell, I'll do my best to oblige.'

Shaken by the undercurrents of barely restrained violence she sensed in him, she retorted, 'That way at least I'll keep my self-respect.'

'We'll see, shall we?'

There was a tacit threat in the softly spoken words that terrified her, and her blood seemed to turn to ice in her veins. Realising she'd pushed him too far, she began, 'Nick, I...'

But he was gone, the door closing behind him with a decisive click.

Trembling in every limb, she got out of bed and, taking clean undies, a patterned wool dress and a pair of high-heeled court shoes from her case, went into the bathroom.

Strangely, for a man normally so tough and ruthless, Nick had made every effort to keep things from escalating into open warfare. But now, due to her own stupidity, her inability to keep her mouth shut, that very thing had happened, and someone—no, not someone—*she* was liable to get hurt.

As she cleaned her teeth and showered she decided that the only thing to do was to try and cool the situation, and the best way to do that might be to go along with his suggestion of a shopping trip and a look around Boston.

Then, if she agreed to meet him halfway, they might at least establish some kind of uneasy truce and avoid the kind of blow for blow confrontation that had just taken place.

As soon as she was dressed, she twisted her long black hair into a knot and secured it on top of her head, then, her face pale but determined, she set off to face Nick.

She was halfway across the bedroom when she realised that her case and all her other belongings had vanished, and she felt a sudden, inexplicable stab of apprehension.

Don't be a fool, she told herself impatiently. The maid or Mrs Espling must have been up and put everything away.

As she made her way down the stairs Nick appeared in the hall wearing a black leather jacket, with her three-quarter-length coat and shoulder-bag over his arm.

'Excellent timing,' he said smoothly, and, his raw-boned face impassive, he helped her into the coat before handing over her bag.

Either he'd read her mind or he'd decided to make the trip into the centre anyway, she thought with relief as he escorted her out to a high beige and brown four-wheel drive vehicle waiting by the kerb and helped her in.

Though the leather upholstery was extremely comfortable, and the air-conditioned vehicle obviously belonged in the luxury class, it was not as stylish as the sleek car he'd driven previously.

For a while Raine looked out of the window as Nick, his heavy-lidded eyes intent, his profile hard, hawk-like, headed north-west through the picturesque streets of Beacon Hill.

Something in his manner made her wary, and her earlier relief slowly drained away to be replaced by a growing unease as she realised that beneath his veneer of calmness there was still a core of cold, deadly anger.

The silence became nerve-racking, oppressive.

Needing to break it, to establish some kind of contact, she asked the first question that came into her head. 'This isn't your usual car, is it?'

'It's one I bought for winter travelling,' he answered shortly.

'What kind is it?'

'A Cherokee Chief.'

Trying to ignore his cool, intimidating manner, she remarked with determined brightness, 'I just thought that it seemed a strange car to take shopping.'

'We're not going shopping.'

Realising he'd thrown away the kid gloves, her previous apprehension turned into a very real fear. Sharply, she demanded, 'Where *are* we going?'

He glanced at her from beneath long, curly lashes, several shades darker than his hair but tipped with gold. 'On our honeymoon.'

So that was why her case and everything had vanished! The shock was like walking into a plate glass window. Yet she should have seen it coming.

Her heart banging against her ribcage, hoping against hope that she was wrong in her sudden certainty, she croaked, '*Where*?'

A cruel little smile twisted his lips and his dark blue eyes were mocking. 'Guess.'

No, she thought violently, she *couldn't* go back to Owl Creek. Though a year ago it had seemed as close to paradise as she was ever likely to get, now it held memories that she couldn't bear to relieve.

Panic-stricken, she cried, 'Oh, no, Nick...' Then, in desperation, 'I'd rather go *anywhere* but there...'

'You had the chance to choose,' he reminded her remorselessly as they crossed the Charles River and headed for the I95 that ran up the New England coast to Maine, 'and you said one hell was as good as another. So, my darling wife, hell is what I intend to make it.'

Raine shuddered violently, but, well aware that she'd brought it on herself, she bit her lip and remained silent.

'Aren't you going to plead with me?' he queried sardonically.

'Would it do any good?'

'No, but I'd derive great satisfaction from hearing you beg.'

One of Margo's expressions popped into Raine's mind, and without stopping to think she snapped, 'On your bike!'

To her surprise he laughed, and sounding grimly amused he remarked, 'I like a touch of spirit. It promises to make taming you all the more enjoyable, and when I've succeeded—'

'What makes you think you'll succeed?' She tried to fight back.

Smiling, he flicked the whip. 'Up at Owl Creek we'll be completely alone—not another soul within miles...'

'You're trying to frighten me,' she accused him hoarsely.

He slanted her a glance. 'And succeeding, by the look on your face.'

After a moment he added silkily, 'But it's too soon to start worrying. Sit back and relax. It'll take approximately five hours to drive up to Bangor, and then some time after that to reach our destination.'

Thinking of the lonely roads that were only used by logging trucks, of the wildness and desolation, she objected anxiously, 'But surely it will be dark long before we get there?'

He shrugged, drawing her unwilling attention to the width of his shoulders.

Memory spotlighted those shoulders, bare and gleaming,

poised above her, recalled the driving force of his body, her own little cries of ecstasy...

Clenching her hands until the nails bit painfully into her palms, she heard him answer laconically, 'We have good lights, and I'm used to the backwoods.'

That fact never failed to surprise her. He always seemed so sophisticated, so much the city-dweller. Yet her uncle Harry had told her that as a young man Nick had spent a lot of time in the lumber camps, developing muscles, building up a magnificent physique with hard, grinding labour, and earning the respect of his future employees by the sweat of his brow.

Harry, too, had loved the outdoors, and in years gone by the pair of them had spent a lot of time trekking and canoeing in the wilderness.

Wilderness... The emotive word made a shudder run through her.

Gathering her courage, she reminded herself that she had five hours. If, during that time, she could find some way of changing his mind, some way of persuading him to stay in Bangor for the night, his anger might evaporate by morning.

'Plotting something?' he enquired softly.

Feeling her face grow hot, she was glad he was looking straight ahead. 'I was wondering why you're going by road,' she said mendaciously. 'I mean, why not by air as we...as we did last time.'

'We could have got a flight to Bangor, but the company plane is in use.'

'What is it normally used for?'

'To ferry people into and out of places inaccessible by road.'

'Who usually flies it?' She needed to keep him talking, to thaw some of that icy anger.

'Bruno Osvald, the company pilot. And Finn and myself when we're up there.'

He was civil, just, but it was obvious that he was in no

mood for conversation, and after several more fruitless attempts she gave it up and relapsed into silence.

Despite her long sleep she must have dozed, because she opened heavy lids to find the calm, sunny weather had been left behind them. A gusty wind was whipping the treetops into a frenzy while rain fell from a grey, turbulent sky.

They had left the I95 and were drawing into a busy shopping complex with a central mall, car parking areas, a large petrol station, a car-rental agency, several steamy diners, a coffee-bar, a drive-through McDonalds and a couple of sea-food restaurants.

'Ready for something to eat?' Nick asked, his voice neutral, neither friendly nor unfriendly.

Though far from hungry, she nodded eagerly. Surely over a meal she would be able to get him to talk, dissipate some of his anger?

And when he showed signs of softening she would suggest an overnight stop in Bangor, then, tomorrow morning, she would put forward Niagara Falls—where there were hotels and people—as a possible honeymoon destination...

But for the moment Bangor represented safety. If they once left the town behind them and headed north-east into the backwoods she would be trapped—alone with Nick and completely at his mercy.

CHAPTER SEVEN

NICK found a parking space near the Lobster Pot, and hurried her the short distance through the pouring rain.

Once inside they were divested of their coats, which were hung on a rail, and shown to a table on a glassed-in veranda with a sandy floor and enough artificial rocks, wicker cages and strange green plants to make an imitation sea-bed.

The place was full of the sound of rain beating against the panes and sluicing down the glass in never-ending streams.

A young, tousle-headed waitress came up, pad and pencil at the ready. She wore an immaculate white blouse, a short black skirt and sneakers. A student working her way through college, Raine guessed.

As the name of the restaurant indicated, the speciality was lobster, and the girl began to reel off the various ways they could be served.

Feeling unable to cope with lobster, Raine shook her head and, after a cursory glance at the menu, with too much on her mind to worry about what she ate, ordered a salad.

As soon as the girl had gone, Raine gathered up her courage and asked in a determinedly casual tone, 'How long will it take to get to Bangor from here?'

'An hour...hour and a half.'

She took a sip of the iced water that seemed a mandatory part of every meal, and suggested, 'You must be getting tired of driving in such awful weather?'

His dark blue eyes showed no sign of softening as they rested on her face, and she sensed with despair that it wasn't going to work. But, anxious at least to buy some time, she forced herself to go on. 'When we get there, wouldn't it make sense to stop at a motel for the night?'

Expression sardonic, he said nothing, and she knew he was dishing out some of her own treatment.

'Wouldn't it?' she pressed. Then, in desperation, 'We could always go on to Owl Creek tomorrow. If you still wanted to...'

Smiling grimly at the rider, he allowed his gaze to travel slowly over her and linger on the swell of her breasts beneath the fine, close-fitting bodice of her dress. 'I'm rather looking forward to getting there tonight,' he said softly, and then he added, 'It wouldn't suit my plans to stay in a motel with people either side and paper-thin walls.'

Though veiled, there was no mistaking the threat.

Watching the shiver that ran though her, he smiled again. His smile wasn't pleasant.

Her heartbeats became irregular, increasing in speed as she contemplated fearfully what lay in store if she didn't manage to change his mind.

But, though he was proud and tough and arrogant, she wouldn't have described him as a vindictive man. So perhaps if she apologised for her earlier behaviour, ate a little humble pie...?

'Nick, I—' She broke off as the waitress returned with her salad and the steak Nick had ordered.

When, the tray tucked under her arm, the girl turned away to take someone else's order, he lifted an enquiring brow at Raine. 'You were saying?'

Knowing how much depended on it, she sought for the right words. 'Earlier you said there was no point in making things worse, and I...I've realised you were quite right.'

His expression cynical, he gave her no encouragement but simply waited, and she swallowed and ploughed on. 'I know I was...unresponsive and difficult. I'm sorry...'

'So you've decided an apology might soften me up?'

Watching the hot colour flood into her cheeks, he informed her trenchantly, 'Well, I'm afraid you're wasting your time.'

'Please, Nick...'

He shook his head. 'Who was it said revenge is sweet?'

'But I—'

'Save your breath and eat,' he advised crisply. 'I want to get on.'

She tried to force down a little of the salad, but, recalling his threat to make their honeymoon hell, she felt sick. Once they were alone, isolated, it would be only too easy to use and humiliate her, strip her of any last shreds of self-respect...

The situation she found herself in was worse than anything she might have imagined, and, fighting against a suffocating panic, she decided that somehow she had to get away.

Once they'd rejoined the interstate he was unlikely to stop again until they'd reached their destination, and then it would be too late.

His own meal finished, Nick frowned at her barely touched plate. 'If you're playing for time...'

'I'm not,' she denied huskily. 'I can't eat any more. But I would like a coffee.'

As soon as their cups were empty he asked the waitress for the bill and paid it, tipping so generously that she looked first taken aback then delighted.

'Gee, thanks! Have a nice day.'

With a hand beneath her elbow, Nick escorted Raine back to the entrance and helped her into her coat.

'I need to wash my hands before we start,' she said, and, pulling away, hurried towards the door marked 'Ladies' Rest Room'.

The air-conditioned unit was pleasant and well lit, with several chairs, a make-up counter and a row of gleaming sinks. The only other occupant was an elderly woman with blue-rinsed hair using the hand drier.

As soon as Raine had the place to herself she took a quick look round; her heart dropped into her shoes. There were no windows in any of the cubicles, and only the one entrance and exit.

Perhaps she could sneak out and, if Nick wasn't in sight, make a run for it...

But he was there, his tall, broad-shouldered figure between her and the outer door. As though some sixth sense had alerted him, he turned as she emerged, and she had no choice but to join him.

Though it was barely mid-afternoon it was almost dark, and raining harder than ever. People hurried to and from their cars huddled beneath umbrellas. Lights spilled from shop windows and flashing neon signs gleamed red and blue and green on the wet paving.

He put his arm around her waist and, ducking their heads, they ran to the four-wheel-drive and scrambled in. As Raine fastened her seat belt raindrops trickled down her face like tears.

Leaning towards her, Nick wiped them away with the back of his hand. Her sharp intake of breath brought a gleam to his eyes, and with a crooked little smile he asked, 'Looking forward to tonight, darling?'

Lips pressed tightly together, she refused to rise to the bait.

They were passing the busy garage on their way back to the interstate when, glancing at the fuel gauge, he said, 'It would make sense to top up on gas before we start.'

One of the pumps became free, and, drawing up in front of it, he switched off the engine and got out.

With a sudden surge of choking excitement, Raine realised that this was the opportunity she needed. The main entrance to the indoor shopping mall wasn't too far away. If she could slip in there it should be comparatively easy to disappear in such a large and bustling complex.

It would mean leaving her case behind, but she would manage somehow. Though she had no dollars, and only a small amount of English money, she had her credit cards.

All she had to do was hide until Nick had given up and gone, then she could hire a car, drive to the nearest motel and lie low until she could decide on the next step.

Not wanting to draw attention to herself, Raine sat quite still, barely breathing, while he filled the tank, replaced the cap and, in order to leave the pump clear, moved the car to a parking bay.

It would make things even easier if this time he left the ignition keys and she could just drive away…

But, as though some warning sense was at work, he took the keys with him as he jumped out once more.

Her heart thudding against her ribs, she watched his black-jacketed figure go into the brightly lit glass-fronted shop and join the straggling queue waiting to pay.

A second later she had unfastened her seat belt and was out of the car, closing the door behind her, so that if he glanced across he'd see nothing amiss.

Knowing it would be a mistake to run, she forced herself to walk away without a backward glance until she could mingle with a little group of shoppers heading for the mall entrance.

Once through the glass doors, heart pounding, legs curiously stiff and alien, Raine hurried along the main concourse, which was swarming with people taking refuge from the rain.

In contrast to the darkness outside it was light and airy, the well-designed central area surrounded by balconies and open to a high roof, giving a feeling of space.

As soon as she was out of sight of the entrance she followed a branch to the left, and halfway along it took an escalator up to the second floor.

Scarcely noticing the trickles of cold water that ran down her neck, she kept walking, putting as much space between herself and possible pursuit as she could.

Many of the shop windows still had striking Hallowe'en displays. But, continually glancing nervously behind her, she scarcely noticed the witches with black steeple hats, the capering goblins, the ghosts trailing white draperies and the orange pumpkins cut into grinning lantern heads.

A glimpse of a tall man with broad shoulders and thick fair hair sent her heart into her mouth. But a second glance showed her that there the similarity ended. He was younger than Nick but several stone overweight, with a fleshy face and a paunch.

Security in the mall was tight, and deliberately obvious. Male and female blue-uniformed guards patrolled, walkie-talkies strapped to their belts. One of them was accompanied by a leashed Alsatian. A youth who was showing signs of being rowdy was separated from his companions and quietly warned.

Feeling vulnerable in the open, Raine followed a couple of well-dressed women into one of the larger departmental stores.

Discovering that to linger aimlessly in any one department for too long brought her suspicious looks from in-store security, she kept moving, mingling with the throng of people. Gradually her nervousness subsided, and she began to feel relatively secure.

After more than an hour of dodging from store to store, Raine told herself firmly that she was safe. Even if Nick had guessed that she'd come in here, it was virtually impossible for one person to search a mall this size. And he wasn't a man to waste time in fruitless endeavour, or to hang about looking a fool.

So, had he given up and gone?

There was only one way to find out.

Lassoing her courage, she went back to the main entrance. It was still pouring, and if anything the wind had heightened, battering signs and awnings and lashing rain into her face.

Keeping under cover as much as possible, she made her

way across to the garage, where strings of multi-coloured flags fluttered wildly. A cautious check of the bay where the four-wheel-drive had been parked showed that it was no longer there.

Breathing a sigh of relief, she hastened into the car rental office and, opening her bag, felt for the wallet containing her credit cards, her driving licence and what little money she had.

Her fingers failed to locate the familiar shape. On stopping to look, she discovered that it appeared to be missing. A second, more thorough and increasingly frantic search only served to confirm that the wallet was definitely gone.

'Can I help you?' a nasal-voiced brunette behind the counter asked.

Completely thrown, Raine stammered, 'I—I wanted to rent a car...but I seem to have lost my wallet.'

'Try asking at the information desk in the mall,' the brunette advised uninterestedly. 'They deal with lost property.'

Turning, Raine blundered out—straight into the arms of a tall, broad-shouldered man whose thick blond hair was beaded with raindrops.

Feeling as though she'd fallen down a lift-shaft, she found herself looking up into Nick's grim, hard-boned face.

'Surprised to see me?' he enquired, his voice as abrasively smooth as pumice stone.

'The c-car wasn't there... I—I thought you'd gone,' she stammered foolishly.

'That was what you were supposed to think. Now, if you've had enough fun...'

Beneath his cool veneer she could tell that he was furious as, an arm around her waist, he propelled her back the way she'd come.

She began to shiver—partly with shock, partly with the cold. If only she'd stayed in the mall where she was safe..

Reading her thoughts with his usual nerve-racking ease,

he said, 'If you hadn't emerged when you did, I would have come in and got you.'

'That wouldn't have been as simple as you're trying to make out,' she objected spiritedly. 'In a big, busy place like that how would you have known where to find me?'

A mirthless little smile twisting his lips, he informed her calmly, 'I've known *exactly* where you were for the past hour.'

Endeavouring to repress the sudden conviction that he'd been playing with her from the start, she shook her head. 'I don't see how you could have done. You didn't follow me...?'

'That wasn't necessary.' Feeling the tremors running through her, he said curtly, 'You ought to have a hot coffee before we get on our way.'

Though steamy and somewhat garish, the coffee-bar he steered her to was bright and welcoming, and not overcrowded.

Perhaps it was the nervous excitement that had sapped her strength, but not until she sank onto one of the red plastic benches did Raine realise how utterly exhausted she felt.

Sipping the coffee, which was good and strong and reviving, she asked in a low voice, 'If you didn't follow me, how did you know where I was?'

'I alerted the mall's security staff and gave them your description. Thinking it was some kind of efficiency test, they picked you up within a few minutes and kept tabs on you.'

As she stared at him, mouth slightly open, he added casually, 'You see, I happen to own the company that runs the mall.'

So all the time she had thought herself relatively safe Big Brother's minions had been watching her. How funny... How incredibly funny! Suddenly, as though her overstretched nerves had finally snapped, she began to laugh.

Hearing and reacting to the edge of hysteria in that laughter, he leaned forward and, taking her face between his palms, covered her mouth with his own, stifling the laughter into silence and causing her heart to start to race.

To any casual observer they must look like lovers, she thought, and the thought pierced her.

When he let her go and moved back, she swallowed some more of the coffee, hands unsteady, while she struggled for and found at least a semblance of composure.

As soon as she could trust her voice, she remarked as lightly as possible, 'I hadn't envisaged a shopping mall forming part of your business interests.'

'When the project was only half finished the original developers got into financial difficulties, so I bought them out and took over.'

'You're pretty good at that.' The acid retort was out before she could prevent it. 'I suppose you own the car-hire firm too?'

'Sorry to disappoint you.' His unsparing glance took in her pallor, her shadowed green eyes, the way her flawless skin seemed stretched tight over those marvellous cheekbones. 'What were you planning to do after hiring a car?'

'Stay at a motel until I'd had time to decide on my next move... However, it seems the odds were stacked against me. Apart from anything else, I've somehow managed to lose my wallet and credit cards.'

He clicked his tongue reprovingly. 'Dear, dear! How very careless of you.'

His expression and his mocking words made her stiffen. Recalling how he'd handed her her coat and bag, she said hoarsely, 'But I didn't lose them, did I? *You* took them!'

'That's right,' he admitted calmly.

Seething with indignation, she demanded, 'Why?'

'Do you need to ask?' He sounded bored.

No, she didn't need to ask. He was a man who left nothing to chance, and he'd been covering just this kind of eventuality. Making sure she was dependent on him. Making sure she had no easy way out.

Watching her expressive face mirror her feeling of trapped despair, he ordered shortly, 'Finish your coffee. It's high time we were on our way.'

Trampling on any remaining shreds of pride, she begged, 'Please, Nick...if only you'll take me back to Boston—'

'You'll be ready to toe the line?' At her almost imperceptible nod, he said derisively, 'That offer comes much too late, my darling wife. After you turned down every chance I gave you of improving our relationship, I decided things should be on *my* terms—with no bargaining on your part.'

So she had gained precisely nothing. She was still faced with the same situation which had scared her into trying to run away...

Or a worse one...

Though he was behaving with cool restraint at the moment, later, when they were alone, she would almost certainly have to pay for her abortive attempt at flight.

A hand beneath her elbow, he urged her to her feet. She glanced around, as though to seek help. But there was no help, and she knew it.

She could cause a scene, refuse to go with him. But then what? She was indisputably his wife, and no one would want to get mixed up in something they'd undoubtedly regard as merely a domestic squabble.

With hopelessness came a kind of dull acceptance, and she allowed herself to be hurried through the wind and rain to the Cherokee, which was hidden between a battered pick-up truck and a silver bullet-shaped sports car.

Perhaps due to the appalling conditions, there were remarkably few vehicles on the road as they regained the interstate and headed north.

It was quite dark now, and as soon as they'd left the lights of the mall behind them the car took on all the aspects of a moving prison.

In the glow from the dashboard Nick's profile looked as hard and unyielding as any gaoler's, and once again Raine was filled with dread. If only she hadn't agreed to Nick's abominable bargain...

Even if it had meant leaving the home he loved, her father, had he known the true situation, would never have allowed her to go through with it... But the marriage still hadn't been consummated, so it wasn't too late to call the whole thing off and have it annulled...

Taking a deep breath, she began, 'I know we made a bargain, but—'

'But you've been trying to wriggle out of your side since the moment I put the ring on your finger...'

Unable to deny the charge, she sat silent, feeling the telltale warmth creeping into her face.

'Haven't you, my darling wife?' His contempt unmistakable, he didn't even glance at her.

'It was a terrible mistake,' she faltered. 'I should never have agreed.'

'Well, you did, and now you're stuck with it,' he informed her coldly.

Made reckless by the knowledge that she'd blown her last chance, she struck savagely at his ego. 'So even though the very thought of having you paw me makes me feel sick, you're going to force me to go through with it?'

He appeared unmoved. 'At this stage in the game I have no intention of allowing you to renege.' Softly, menacingly, he added, 'And I intend to do rather more than just "paw" you. Apart from anything else, we've some scores to settle.'

Shuddering inwardly, she relapsed into silence.

The shush of tyres on wet tarmac and the metronome click of the wiper-blades kept her uneasy thoughts company while the road unwound before them like an endless roll of shiny black plastic.

Her heart felt like lead as through the pouring rain their

headlights picked up the signs for Bangor, only to swish past, leaving them in their wake.

On the I95 there had been comparatively little traffic. Now, as they left the interstate and headed north-east towards the Canadian border, there was virtually none.

Any faint hope that he might relent gone, Raine faced the fact that before long they would be at Owl Creek. Then, a virtual prisoner, she would have only two options. She could give in without a struggle, or fight him. But either way the end result would be the same. She would be shamed and humiliated…

Uneasy thoughts fretted her until, lulled by the combination of movement, semi-darkness and comforting warmth, her brain grew muzzy and her eyelids drooped.

Shaken into wakefulness, she opened her eyes to find they were bumping along an ungraded road, little more than a track through the forest. Their lights showed that the rutted surface was a sea of wet mud, and on either side dark dripping pine trees pressed close.

Jolting and slithering, they continued down it for what seemed miles, until the trees opened up and through the rain the Cherokee's headlights picked out the plank bridge that crossed Owl Creek.

The slippery span, just wide enough to accommodate a car, had no guard-rails, and, catching a glimpse of the swollen water swirling and eddying past huge boulders, Raine held her breath. But Nick took them across without hesitation, showing no more concern than if he were driving over Lopsley's Sley Bridge.

He stopped the dirt-spattered four-wheel-drive a short distance from the cabin, and, jumping down, bare-headed in the pouring rain, came round to help her out.

Glancing from the quagmire underfoot to her court shoes, he remarked, 'You'll never make it in those. I'd better carry you.'

Stiffening, she objected sharply, 'I don't want you to carry me. I can manage perfectly well.'

In the light from the dashboard she saw him raise satirical brows, but all he said was, 'As you like.' Holding the door open, he stood back.

Though Raine descended carefully, as soon as she touched the ground her high heels sank deep into the mud. Gritting her teeth, she managed two or three squelching steps before losing first one shoe then the other.

Her stockinged feet failing to get a grip on the surface as slippery as it was uneven, she floundered helplessly and, unable to keep her balance, went sprawling full-length.

Through the noise of the rain she heard Nick's laugh, then he was bending over her, asking with mock solicitude, 'Sure you don't need any help?'

'Quite sure!' she spat at him, struggling to her knees. 'I'll manage if I have to crawl there.'

'Then I'll leave you to it.'

She had barely regained her feet when she measured her length again in the soft mud. Soft mud be blowed! This time there were rocks and roots embedded in it, and she lay for a moment or two partially winded, a pain in her ribs and her right cheek stinging.

As good as his word, however, Nick ignored her while he took her case and his grip from the boot and opened the cabin door.

Furiously, and perhaps unfairly, she mentally consigned him to hell while she collected both herself and her shoulder-bag and made another attempt to rise.

A few seconds later yellow light was shining from the windows, and he returned to douse the headlights and close the car.

By the time Raine had battled her way to the veranda steps, she was covered with mud and soaked through to the skin.

Inside the shelter of the porch the cabin door had been

left open for her, and the place looked just as she remembered.

Recalling the pure joy and bliss she'd found there last time, she had to bite her lip against the pain and remind herself sharply that her happiness had been based on lies and deception. All the time he'd been making love to her, he'd been planning to marry another woman.

Forcing her reluctant legs to carry her across the threshold, she closed the heavy door behind her and hung the strap of her handbag over one of the coat-hooks.

Nick, a matchbox in his hand, was crouching in front of the hearth. As she stood by the door shivering he glanced up.

She was filthy and dishevelled. One cheek was grazed and bleeding, her hair had come loose and was hanging in black rats' tails around her shoulders, her feet and ankles were thickly caked in mud and her right knee was cut where she'd caught the edge of an old tree stump.

Nick's searching gaze travelled slowly over her, before returning to her bloody, mud-streaked face. It was difficult to read his expression.

Waiting for him to gloat, she lifted her chin and braced herself. But, rising to his feet, his voice cool and impersonal, he merely observed, 'It's a pity foolish pride forced you to make such a mess of yourself.'

Trying to ignore the shivers running through her, she shrugged. 'I've always understood that mud's good for the complexion.'

With a gleam of something that could have been reluctant admiration in his eyes, he advised evenly, 'You'd better get out of those wet things.' And added, 'I've lit the heater so there'll be hot water.'

Thick curtains had been drawn across the window, and as well as the water-heater, Nick had lit a radiant heater which was already taking the worst of the chill from the air.

Having stripped off her saturated clothing and bundled

it into a dirty-linen basket, Raine hurriedly removed the last few pins from her hair and stepped under the shower. Though it stung her cheek and knee, the flow of hot water was like a benediction.

A shelf held a wide selection of toilet requisites, including toothpaste, a plastic-wrapped toothbrush and a couple of spare combs.

Needing to wash her hair, she reached for the shampoo. It had a clean, tangy scent, the subtle fragrance of spruce that always hung around Nick.

Things were bad enough without her having to *smell* like him, she thought vexedly. But, even if she'd been in a state to search through her case, her own toilet bag was almost certainly still in the bathroom at Mecklenburg Place.

In a cupboard above the heater were facecloths, piles of towels and a couple of white bathrobes. Clean once more, her hair rubbed almost dry and a comb pulled through it, she donned one of the towelling robes and, having belted it tightly and turned the sleeves up several times, ventured forth.

The stove was blazing merrily now, and the air felt appreciably warmer. The closed curtains shut out the inclement night and helped to make the place cosy.

Nick was just coming in with an armful of wood from the covered store on the veranda. Judging by how wet his hair was, and the pile of logs stacked alongside the stove, he'd made the same journey several times before. He'd also rescued her abandoned shoes. They stood in the hearth, mud-covered and forlorn.

Shrugging out of his leather jacket, he hung it next to her handbag and queried, 'Feeling OK now?'

She nodded.

Suddenly he was much too close, only inches away, looking down into her beautiful face. Brushing aside a strand of black silky hair, he clicked his tongue over the graze on her cheek. Then tenderly, as though she were a child, he bent to kiss it better.

When she flinched away from him, his mouth tightened ominously, but all he said was, 'I take it you've finished in the bathroom?'

'Yes.'

'Then I'm going to have a shower. You can begin your wifely duties by getting a meal ready.'

Infuriated by his mocking command, she stared at him in sullen silence.

He sighed. 'Surely you can open a can?'

'Quite certain you don't want me to go out and shoot something fresh?'

He laughed as if genuinely amused, his face devilishly attractive above the black polo-necked sweater, and, looking from the spotless robe to her bare feet, he shook his head. 'Not dressed like that. As you may have noticed, it's a little muddy.'

When she bit her lip, he gave her a taunting smile, and turning towards the bathroom said derisively, 'If you can't manage anything better, I'll settle for baked beans.'

If she couldn't manage anything better than baked beans, indeed! Fuming, she opened her case and put on fresh undies, a pair of trousers, an aubergine-coloured boat-necked jumper that fastened down the front with small pearl studs and, blessing Martha's foresight, a pair of furry slippers.

The larder was as well stocked as it had been on her previous visit and, still muttering imprecations, she began to collect together the ingredients for a slap-up meal. She'd show the clever devil just what she *could* manage.

CHAPTER EIGHT

WHEN, some ten minutes later, Nick emerged from the bathroom fully dressed but still towelling his thick wheat-coloured hair, she was so engrossed in her task that she barely glanced in his direction.

As soon as the main course was ready, and the apple pie's pastry turning crisp and golden, she set the table and dished up while Nick opened a bottle of Californian Chenin Blanc and filled two glasses.

The outer ring of rice was light and fluffy, cooked to perfection, the tinned chicken and vegetables with little curls of smoked ham and artichoke hearts fresh-looking and colourful, the herbs and spices mouth-wateringly aromatic.

As he regarded the offering appreciatively she reached for a jug keeping warm on the stove and told him, 'All it needs now is the finishing touch.'

'It looks and smells delicious,' he commented.

'I'm *so* glad you approve.'

Alerted by the dulcet tones, he shot her a wary glance.

In return she gave him an innocent smile and, tilting the jug, covered rice and chicken alike with a rich, creamy sauce, saying, 'You'll find this is special.'

The cheese sauce was a fairly ordinary one out of a jar. What made it special was the liberal amount of strong yellow washing-up liquid she'd added.

Her face guileless, Raine picked up a serving spoon and helped Nick, then herself. She was sipping her wine when he took his first mouthful.

The fork clattered onto the plate and, lips clamped together, he headed for the bathroom while she continued to sit and sip from her glass.

It was several minutes later before he emerged looking dangerously calm. Coming to stand over her, he said softly, almost admiringly, 'You little cat.'

As though they were carrying on a quite normal conversation, she said, 'There's a pie in the oven.'

'What's that got in it?' he enquired interestedly.

'Nothing. It's a perfectly good apple pie.'

'Well, strange as it may appear, I don't seem to fancy food any longer. In fact—' his voice became a purr '—I think I'll indulge a different kind of appetite.'

'No!' she exclaimed sharply. 'I won't let you just use me.'

'How do you plan to stop me?'

Biting her lip, she remained silent while thoughts ricocheted in her mind. She couldn't stop him... He was so much stronger than she was... But he wasn't the kind of man who would enjoy making love to a reluctant woman, so her one hope might be to freeze him off...

As though she'd spoken her thoughts aloud, he said evenly, 'If you were intending to try giving me a cool reception, I'm warning you it won't work.'

'Then I'll struggle!'

He laughed, his white teeth gleaming. 'How melodramatic.'

'I mean it. You'll have to use force.'

'We'll see, shall we?'

His hand beneath her elbow, he urged her to her feet and away from the kitchen. Hanging back, wishing, now it was too late, that she hadn't precipitated matters, she stammered, 'I—I was going to make a pot of coffee.'

'Stalling?'

'No,' she lied hastily, 'I'd really like some.'

He looked impatient. About to refuse.

'Surely you could do with a cup? And I'm thirsty...

Please...' Hating herself for begging, and him for making her, still she sought to put off the evil moment.

'Very well,' he said evenly. 'But this is the last delaying tactic I shall tolerate.' Steering her towards the comfortable circle of glowing warmth cast by the stove, he pushed her into one of the low armchairs. 'And as for the coffee, *I'll* make it.' His smile lopsided, he added, 'You might know where the rat poison's kept.'

'If I did I'd have used it earlier,' she retorted.

While he boiled the water and filled the cafetière Raine stared into the leaping flames and faced the fact that all she'd succeeded in buying was a little time, not a reprieve.

He fully intended to make love to her, and while her body would delight in it, her heated flesh come alive at his touch, because he felt nothing for her but desire, her heart would grow cold and die.

With a kind of numb detachment she watched the wood in the stove settle and send up a shower of bright crackling sparks. The scent of burning fir logs was sharp and resinous, mingling with the fragrant smell of coffee. Rain beat against the windows and gusts of wind buffeted the cabin and soughed through the pines while, chills running through her, all thought suspended now, she waited like a victim on the steps of the guillotine.

The coffee, when it came, was accompanied by a bottle of cognac and two glasses. Putting the tray on a small table, Nick pressed the cafetière plunger and poured the steaming brew before dropping into the chair opposite.

Firelight gleamed in his dark eyes and shone on his face, picking out the strong planes and angles and making his bronze skin look ruddy. 'Brandy?' he queried.

Sipping her coffee, she hesitated.

'A little might help to relax you,' he suggested blandly.

About to refuse, she changed her mind and nodded. If she drank enough it might provide some Dutch courage... Or serve as a kind of anaesthetic for what was to come...

This time there was no possibility of escape, and she knew it.

She recalled her own defiant, You'll have to use force, and his dry, 'We'll see, shall we?' He hadn't said he wasn't prepared to, and her earlier conviction that he wouldn't want to make love to a reluctant woman had evaporated.

He poured a minimal amount of cognac, rather than the generous measure she'd been expecting, and passed it to her.

When she lifted the glass to her lips her hand was shaking so much that it chinked against her teeth. She swallowed the amber liquid down as though it were medicine, and held out the glass for more.

He refused to give her any more. 'I think not. Since breakfast you've had scarcely anything to eat, so it will go straight to your head.'

'I don't care.'

'Well, I do,' he said evenly, taking the glass from her hand. 'I don't intend to have you flaking out on me. We've all the night before us—' his smile was full of meaning, filled with lazy anticipation '—and I promised you a long, slow seduction.'

Panic brought her to her feet.

Before she could make any move to escape, he was looming over her. Running his fingers into her silky black hair, he held her face between his palms, his thumbs stroking erotically over her high cheekbones.

When she stood quite still, gazing up at him with wide green eyes, he bent his head and began to cover her face with thistledown kisses. Kisses sweeter than wine.

His lips, teasing and tantalising, closed her eyelids, brushed her brows, touched the tip of her nose and then lingered briefly at the corner of her mouth before moving away to follow the clean line of chin and jaw.

'I've waited a long time for this,' he whispered huskily, 'and I want you to be aware and responsive while I'm making love to you.'

Punctuating each sentence with a series of sensuous kisses, he went on, 'I want to watch your face while I wring every last ounce of pleasure from your body... I want to feel the shudders of ecstasy running through you... I want to hear your little gasps and moans... And finally, when you can't bear any more of such exquisite torture, I want to hear you beg...'

Raine's heart beat so suffocatingly fast that she found it hard to breathe—and even harder to subdue her treacherous body's yearnings and awakening hunger.

Somehow, she said, 'If you'd like to hear me beg, I'll do it now. Please let me go, Nick. I should never have agreed to this marriage. I don't want you to make love to me...'

Even before she'd finished speaking she knew it was futile. There was no compassion, no hint of softening in that hard, arrogantly handsome face.

'Then, my darling, I must decide how best to change your mind. It's high time you were my wife in the fullest sense of the word.'

Through stiff lips, she said, 'I'd find being your wife degrading.'

She saw the sudden flare of anger in those midnight-blue eyes and knew that the word 'degrading' had struck home.

Smiling like a tiger, he said silkily, 'Don't worry, I'll make sure you enjoy your *degradation*.'

One hand moved to support the back of her head while the other curved itself around her throat and stroked gently up and down. Staring at him like a mesmerised rabbit, she swallowed convulsively.

Holding her eyes, he followed the elegant length of her throat with a fingertip before slipping his hand into the boat-neck of her jumper.

The muscular wrist, with its sprinkling of golden hair, rested against the top button and exerted just enough pressure to make the pearl stud pull out of the buttonhole.

His fingers slid into her low-cut bra, splaying over the warm curve of her breast, stroking lightly, feeling her nipple grow firm in response to his touch.

Desire kicked low in her stomach, and she sucked air into her lungs like a swimmer who had been under water too long.

He smiled, and his little finger and thumb spanned from nipple to nipple. The second stud pulled free. Bending his head, he touched his lips to the hammering pulse at the base of her throat while his fingers dealt with the remaining buttons and the front fastening of her flimsy bra. In a moment he had deftly slipped both garments from her shoulders and tossed them aside.

She felt his lips on the pale satiny skin of her breast, and then the dampness of his tongue circling the dusky peak, and she shuddered in anticipation.

But, instead of the promised delight, all at once he was drawing away, pulling his black sweater over his head and discarding it.

Her eyes were riveted to the masculine perfection of his naked torso, the strong column of his throat, the sculptured grace of wide shoulders tapering to a narrow waist and lean hips.

His chest was broad, the clear, healthy skin like oiled silk over the plates of muscle layering the ribcage. He was carrying not an ounce of spare flesh, and the bunched power of his shoulders and biceps told of his superb fitness and strength. A fine sprinkle of golden hair arrowed in a V towards the waistband of his trousers.

'Touch me,' he suggested softly. 'You know you want to.'

Last time a certain shyness had inhibited her, but now she wanted more than anything in the world to touch him. But once she did she would be lost…

As she stared, dry-mouthed, he took her hands and placed the palms against his chest, imprisoning them there when a reflex action would have made her snatch them away.

When he released his hold for a moment she stood quite still, then, with a revealing little sigh, closed her eyes and began a tactile journey.

Lack of vision concentrated and intensified the pleasure, and she found a sensual delight in the crisp whorls of hair beneath her fingertips, the exciting prickle against her palms.

She stroked across the silken skin of his shoulders and exulted in the smooth ripple of muscles as his hands went out to span her slim waist. Discovering the small flat nipples, she allowed her tongue to explore their leathery texture.

Her breath was warm and damp against his chest, and fine strands of silky black hair clung like a spider's web. She bit him delicately, and in response to the shudder that shook him felt a quick surge of triumph at knowing how strongly she could affect him.

His skin tasted faintly salty, and the scent of spruce and fresh perspiration proved to be a potent aphrodisiac.

So intent was she that she scarcely noticed when he undid her trousers and eased them over the swell of her hips. A second later her dainty panties followed. At his urging she stepped forward, leaving the garments and her slippers behind.

Cupping her bare buttocks, he pressed the lower half of her body firmly to his. Her breasts brushed against his hair-roughened chest and her nipples sprang into aching life.

She made a small, inarticulate sound, and as if in answer he guided her hands to the clip on the waistband of his trousers.

Her unfed sensual hunger was so urgent, so demanding that her fingers fumbled, hardly able to perform their task.

Refusing to give her any further help, he waited until she'd unfastened the zip and slid both trousers and briefs down over his lean hips. Then, pulling off his shoes and socks, he pushed the small pile of clothing aside.

Just for a moment he allowed her to touch and stroke the firm flesh she had freed, then, sweeping her off her feet, he pulled a cushion from the settee for her head to rest on and, as he had done once before, laid her on the thick bearskin rug in front of the stove.

Standing looking down, he let his gaze travel slowly over her. She lay with her eyes closed, her black hair spilling over the bright cushion. Her beautifully shaped breasts were high and firm, her creamy skin—made rosy by the firelight—flawless, her slender body long-legged and graceful.

'You're even lovelier than I remember,' he murmured huskily. Stretching out beside her, propped on one elbow, he put a palm against her cheek and ordered, 'Look at me, Raine.'

Long black lashes flickered, and she stared up into his hard-boned face, her eyes still molten with sensual feeling.

Softly, he said, 'I've been under your spell from the first moment I saw you...'

But the spell was mutual...

'I couldn't get you out of my mind.' He ran a thumb over the lovely curve of her lips. 'You completely enchanted me...'

But he'd still gone ahead and married another woman... The thought formed in her mind, clear and cold as ice crystals.

'My green-eyed witch...' His voice sank to a whisper. Lifting her hands, he kissed each palm. 'Tell me you want me as much as I want you...'

She tried to deny that she wanted him, but her body was on fire, as though with fever, and her throat was so dry she couldn't speak.

Her eyes dropped to the firm line of his lips. He bent his head and kissed her. As though there was no help for it, her mouth opened to the demand of his.

While he deepened the kiss he began to caress her, feather-light touches that brought to life every sensor in her skin.

He was a gentle, unhurried lover, his hands tantalising and tormenting her, learning every quivering inch, driving her slowly wild, making her his before he actually took her.

When his mouth followed his hands down to her breasts and he began to tease the eager nipples with lips and teeth and tongue, the needle-sharp sensations were so piercingly sweet that she gasped and moaned, unsure how much she could bear of such exquisite torment.

While he suckled at one breast and his thumb delicately stimulated the other rosy peak his free hand roved over the silken skin of her inner thigh. Finding its goal unerringly, the pressure of a single finger evoked such an explosion of feeling that she bucked and writhed and whimpered.

Withdrawing a little, he asked softly, 'Do you want me to make love to you, Raine?'

Her arms went around his neck to pull him to her with a wordless, hungry passion that told him all he needed to know.

Still he held back. 'Say it,' he ordered. 'I want to hear you say it.'

'Yes—yes, I want you to make love to me,' she cried hoarsely, and again tried to pull him to her.

He laughed softly, mocking her eagerness. 'Gently, darling. There's no hurry. We've got all the night before us, and there are a lot of exquisite sensations you still haven't experienced…'

When Raine awoke she was snuggled in a comfortable cocoon of warmth and darkness broken only by a faint red glow from the stove on the far side of the room.

Her body felt vital and alive, yet full of a languorous lethargy, while her mind was stupefied, dazed and disorientated, as though she was a survivor of some disaster.

It was a moment or two before her head cleared and recollection came flooding back like a tide, carrying with it memories of lovemaking that made her whole body flush with heat.

They were in bed now, lying spoon-fashion, Nick's hard length at her back, the weight of his arm across her ribcage and his hand cupped possessively around her breast. She could just make out his quiet, even breathing.

Oh, but his strategy had been brilliant! Looking back, she could see how he had led her every step of the way. And she had gone like a lamb to the slaughter.

He had done everything that he'd said he wanted to do. Including making her beg. Although his domination had been a silken one, he had proved himself her master from start to finish—treating her, *playing* with her as though she was a toy.

All memory of the pleasure he had given her was wiped out. Bitterly she cursed her own lack of self-control. Despite repeated warnings to herself, in the end she had made no attempt either to struggle or to freeze him off. And she hadn't only submitted, she had been willing, eager…

She felt desperately ashamed and humiliated. If only she'd put up a fight, made it necessary for him to use force, then at least she could have faced him with her head held high and lived with herself.

Now she could do neither. She had allowed herself to be the plaything of a man who had no feelings for her except anger and lust.

Lust… An ugly word for a powerful emotion. An emotion which a year ago, in her innocence, she had believed to be love. That mistake had made her subsequent disillusionment all the harder to bear.

If she had been a more sophisticated woman, or if she hadn't loved him so very much, she might have been able to look on their brief liaison as a pleasurable interlude and put the whole thing down to experience, rather than allowing pain and anger to stampede her into running away.

But she hadn't. And, in its own way, Nick's reaction had proved to be as extreme as her own.

Because of her flight, her refusal to see or listen to him—and in spite of being engaged to a woman he loved—he had become obsessed with her.

It was an obsession which, though he'd gone to extreme lengths to gratify it, he obviously resented as bitterly as she resented the hold he had over her.

So where did that leave them?

Presumably he expected them to stay married until his obsession was cured—an open-ended sentence, she'd called it—and then he would let her go. But by that time she could be destroyed, burnt out…

A kind of panicky nausea gripped her.

Nick was still breathing with the shallow evenness of sleep as, her empty stomach churning, she carefully eased herself free of his imprisoning arm and crept across the darkened room to the bathroom.

The stove had been closed up for the night, and as soon as Raine left the warmth of the bed the cold air wrapped around her like an invisible shroud, goose-fleshing her bare skin.

Taut and shivering, she leaned over the sink and waited until the nausea had subsided. Then, clenching her teeth to stop them chattering, she tiptoed back through the darkness to huddle by the stove, legs drawn up, arms hugging them, cheek resting against her knees.

'What the *hell* are you doing?' She hadn't heard him coming, and the savage question startled her, jerking her head up.

In the faint glow from the stove she saw he was standing over her, naked and furious. 'You'll catch your death of cold, you silly little fool.'

'I—I felt a bit sick.'

His voice softened with what sounded like concern. 'It's probably lack of food. I'll get you some biscuits and hot chocolate.'

Her stomach kicked at the thought. 'No, no… I don't want anything.'

'Then come back to bed.'

When she made no move to obey he stooped and, gathering her into his arms, carried her back to the bed. Slipping in beside her, he drew her against his chest, holding her protectively, warming her shivering body with his own.

Soon the shaking stopped and a comforting warmth began to steal over her, but, telling herself how much she hated the contact, she made an effort to stay rigid. Before long, however, her spine began to protest at the unnatural strain, and she was forced to let herself relax against him.

'That's better,' he said softly, and, turning a little, so that she was sprawled half across his chest, settled his chin on top of her head.

Beneath her cheek his heartbeat was strong and steady, oddly reassuring. Moments later she was asleep.

She awoke to find daylight poking fingers through slight gaps in the curtains and Nick propped on one elbow, his thickly-lashed midnight-blue eyes smiling down at her. His wheat-coloured hair was rumpled, and a silvery-gold stubble adorned his strong jaw.

He was so attractive, so irresistible when he smiled like that, that her heart gave a queer little lurch and began to flap about like a stranded fish.

Perhaps something of what she was feeling showed in her face, because his smile deepened, grew satisfied.

He bent and touched his lips to hers, his breath warm and sweet. 'Last night—the way you responded to me—was everything I could have wished for…' He kissed her again. 'It convinced me that you must have felt something other than hatred…'

Her defence mechanism sprang into action. 'Oh, I did,' she said quickly. 'Lust.' She almost laughed at his expression. 'Lust isn't just a male prerogative. Women feel it too—or didn't you know?'

He answered obliquely. 'I've nothing against good honest passion, but in your case I thought your feelings went deeper than that?'

As she began to shake her head he said positively, 'You loved me once, otherwise you would never have dropped all your defences like you did...'

Unable to deny that, she looked at him dumbly.

'I wondered if by any chance you still loved me?'

The question was like a knife thrust into her heart and twisted. Conscious only of the pain, she hit back blindly, *wanting* to hurt him. 'What makes you think I could love a man who's made me into a whore?'

He flinched, and she laughed bitterly. 'Too crude for you? But that's what it amounts to.'

'Don't be foolish, Raine—'

'But perhaps a whore's better off,' she broke in heedlessly. 'At least she can *choose* who she sells her body to.'

'We're married,' he pointed out tightly, 'with all that implies. *You're my wife*.'

'Under duress.' Her green eyes blazed. 'You once said that all you wanted from me was the use of my body, and that's all you'll ever get! Not comfort or concern if you're injured or ill, not help and support when you're tired and you need a shoulder to lean on, not compassion if your world falls apart, not even true companionship...

'*Love* you?' She laughed scornfully. 'I *loathe* you! If you were up to your neck in quicksand I wouldn't lift a finger to help—in fact I'd stand and cheer while you went under.'

His face a stony mask, a white line around his mouth, he said, 'There's no need to say any more. You've made your feelings abundantly clear. And if all I'm to ever get is *the use of your body*—' his words dropped into the silence like slivers of ice '—then I'll have to make the most of it.'

His mouth a thin, cruel line, he put his hand on her breast and fingered the nipple with cool insolence, before running the hand down her body to find an even more sensitive spot.

There was no tenderness in his touch, no passion, even. He was treating her with studied contempt, waiting for her to react, she thought bitterly, hoping she would struggle so he could hurt her.

Breathing with slow, deliberate care, she lay quite still, her face deathly pale and calm, her teeth clenched on the soft ski of her inner lip to stop it trembling. Aided by a kind of icy despair, she struggled to show no reaction, to allow no flicker of emotion to break through that unresponsive mask.

Watching him from beneath thick lashes, she saw, first with wonder then with a feeling of triumph, that of the two of them he was growing more aroused.

A flicker of angry impatience showed briefly in his dark eyes, and he took her hand and placed it on his firm flesh.

She let it stay there, limp and unmoving, with a mute unconcern that was in itself an insult, a blow to his manhood.

His lips twisted. 'If you're going to liken yourself to a bought woman, darling, you'll have to make more effort to please.' Savagely, derisively, he added, 'Somersby would no doubt have been satisfied with making love to someone who lay there like a corpse, but—'

For some reason his jeer got through her guard, and with no thought for the possible consequences she lashed out, the palm of her hand cracking against his cheek with a force that made him blink.

Unbelievably, he laughed.

That mocking laughter made her see red. Hands curved into claws, she went for him like a tigress, scratching and biting with a primitive fury that later she would be ashamed of.

'Ouch! You little hellcat!' he exclaimed as she sank her teeth into his shoulder. His attention distracted, she scrambled for the opposite edge of the bed, and had almost reached it when he seized her and dragged her back, struggling furiously.

As he attempted to restrain her her flailing fist caught him a glance blow on the cheek, and she heard his little grunt of pain with fierce satisfaction.

Her satisfaction was short-lived. A moment later he had grasped her wrists and, using the weight of his body to hold hers down, pinioned her arms above her head.

He took her then, without any preliminaries and with a disregard for her as a woman that was little short of brutal.

But her emotions were running at fever-pitch, and she met his anger with anger and his passion with an equal and matching passion that sent them plunging into a fiery volcano.

For perhaps the first time in his adult life Nick lost his magnificent control, and in losing it found a depth of satisfaction that he'd never experienced before.

Afterwards he lay with his head heavy on her breast while their heartbeats and breathing slowed to a more normal rate.

When he lifted himself away she was already fast asleep, beautiful lips slightly parted, long black lashes lying like fans on her cheeks, one outflung hand resting palm uppermost by her dark head.

He gazed down at her, a look on his face that would have transfixed her had she seen it—a mingling of anger and pain and tenderness, and something more than tenderness.

With a sigh he gathered her into his arms, and, having kissed her softly, pulled the duvet over their sweat-slicked bodies and settled down to watch her sleep.

Some time later, half-asleep and half-awake, she stirred and stretched, the movement causing a draught of chill air. With an incoherent murmur, she ducked her head and snuggled closer to the comforting warmth that wrapped around her.

A living warmth. She opened her eyes to find that her

nose was pressed against Nick's muscular chest. When she moved, the contact with his hair-roughened skin caused her to sneeze.

The explosive little sound made him laugh. He had a pleasant laugh, deep and masculine, a laugh that rumbled in his chest and made her want to laugh with him.

But she had nothing to laugh about.

Remembering the wildness of their coming together, and what had gone before, she went hot and cold. Drawing away, she looked at him.

There were scratches on his face and what looked like the beginning of a bruise beneath his left eye. On his shoulder she could see a set of marks, angry reddish purple against the smooth bronze skin.

Following her gaze, he said, 'Yes…'

Shame filled her and she flushed scarlet. She had acted like an alley cat.

'But don't blame yourself too much. You had plenty of provocation.'

Deliberate provocation, no doubt. But even that didn't excuse the way she had behaved.

'I'm sorry,' she said quietly.

'Does that mean you're willing to call a truce and try to enjoy our honeymoon?'

'You said you intended to make it hell,' she reminded him.

'I said a lot of things when I was angry,' he admitted wryly. 'But I'll be happy to settle for a spot of peaceful coexistence.'

Nothing that had been said altered the basic situation, or the way she felt about things, but she'd been badly shocked and frightened by her own lack of control, and she doubted if her abused nervous system could take any more at the moment.

Dark blue eyes looked into green. 'Pax?'

She knew that the peaceful coexistence Nick had proposed wasn't enough. It might make the immediate present slightly more bearable, but to save herself from becoming a burnt-out shell she had to get away from him at the very first opportunity.

He lifted her chin. 'Well, Raine?'

'Pax,' she agreed, and hoped that on this occasion he couldn't read her thoughts.

CHAPTER NINE

APPARENTLY he couldn't. The tension died out of his face. Looking suddenly happy, almost carefree, he kissed her lightly on the lips and said, 'The kiss of peace... Now, you stay where you are while I warm the place up.'

He got out of bed and crossed the room with the unconscious pantherish grace that characterised all his movements. Opening the stove, he stirred the embers into life before piling on split wood and several good-size logs.

Leaning back against her pillows, the duvet pulled up to her chin, Raine watched him covertly.

When he drew back the curtains she saw that the previous night's storm had passed. The day was fine, the lake calm and the sky a clear bright blue.

As he stood by the window, quite unselfconscious about his nakedness, sunlight poured in, turning his bronzed body to gold.

Oh, but he was breathtaking, beautiful as Apollo, with a magnificent male beauty that made her throat go dry and every nerve in her body grow tense.

When he turned to smile at her she observed, her voice a little squeaky, 'It's a good thing we haven't any neighbours.'

He chuckled. 'Well, not close ones. Apart from an occasional hiker camping in the woods, our nearest neighbours are Kurt and Lisbet Doody. They have a cabin across the lake. They're nice folks.

'When they realise we're here they might come over to

say hi…' His eyes on her face, he went on, 'Or after breakfast maybe we could go and call on them?'

Painfully aware that they must both look as if they'd been in the wars, she didn't relish the thought of meeting his friends. It didn't seem to bother *him*, however, so, squaring her shoulders, she answered as cheerfully as possible. 'If that's what you want to do.'

But, picking up the lack of enthusiasm in her tone, he said mildly, 'We don't have to; it was merely a suggestion… So, any ideas on what you *would* like to do today? Walking? Canoeing?'

Raine knew from her last visit that a tarpaulined two-man canoe was stowed under the veranda, and she loved being out of the lake, but at the moment she felt more like stretching her legs.

Before she could answer, he suggested hopefully, with a gleam in his eye, 'Unless, of course, you'd prefer to spend the day in bed?'

Hurriedly, she said, 'I could do with some exercise.'

His lifted brow made her blush scarlet.

'*Outdoor* exercise,' she emphasised tartly.

'Pity.' Grinning at her discomfort, he collected an armful of clothes and headed for the bathroom.

By the time he emerged, wearing casual cords and an olive-green turtle-necked sweater, his still damp hair a dark blond, the air was comfortably warm.

While Raine took a leisurely shower, letting the hot water run over a body which felt stiff but at the same time glowingly alive, Nick opened a carton of orange juice and prepared breakfast.

Sitting in front of the stove, they tucked in hungrily to platefuls of tinned sausages, beans and chunks of the malted fruity brown bread that on first acquaintance Raine had wrinkled her nose at, but which she now loved. They finished off with mugs of coffee and huge slices of cold apple pie.

Replete, she sat back with a sigh while Nick poured more coffee.

When their mugs were empty again, he asked, 'Ready for that exercise you mentioned?'

'I'm not sure I can move.'

'Come on, lazybones.' Taking her hand, he pulled her to her feet. 'I'll try to choose a route that's not too muddy, but just in case there are spare boots with the outdoor gear on the porch. And we'll have to make sure we're visible,' he added. 'It's the start of the hunting season.'

When, following Nick's example, she'd put on boots and a warm anorak with an orange waistcoat, he dropped a bright orange hat on her head and said, 'You'll do.'

Considering the amount of rain that had fallen, the mud wasn't as bad as she'd feared, and by the lake the rocky uneven ground was covered with a brown carpet of pine needles, which were pleasantly springy underfoot.

A cold, bright front had followed the storm, and the sunny air was crisp and sparkling, making the walk along the lakeshore most enjoyable.

Coming to a halt, Nick put an arm around her waist and, drawing her back against him, with his free hand pointed across the lake to the opposite shore. 'See over there...?'

A low frame-built house nestled amongst the trees, blue smoke rising from its chimney. Suddenly flustered by his nearness, the effect he had on her, she nodded without speaking.

'That's the Doodys' place.'

Needing something to say, she asked, 'Do they live there permanently?' and wondered fleetingly how they made a living.

'Yes. Have done for years.' Answering her unspoken query, he went on, 'Kurt is a writer and Lisbet keeps horses. Sometimes I take up their offer of the loan of a mount... Do you ride?'

'I'm not really a horsewoman, but I enjoy going out with Margo from time to time.'

'Perhaps tomorrow, if it's fine, we could ride over to Saskis Pond, where there's a beaver lodge? We may be lucky enough to see one of its inhabitants.'

'Oh, I'd like that,' she said eagerly.

'Then after breakfast I'll drive round to the Doodys and borrow a couple of horses.' Leaning forward a shade, he dipped his head so that his cold cheek rested against hers. 'If you fancy the idea, we could take a picnic in our saddlebags.'

'That would be nice.' She tried to answer calmly, but her heart was racing and her normally low-pitched voice sounded high and a little breathless.

She thought he might be going to kiss her, but after a moment he straightened up and they moved on.

Feeling both regret and relief, she asked herself crossly how it was that another human being could affect her so strongly.

The very fact that he *did* made it all the more imperative to get away as soon as possible, before she found herself unable to go, caught and trapped in a silken web of allure like a fly in a spider's web...

Deep in thought, she tripped over a root, and Nick had to catch her arm to save her falling.

'It pays to watch where you're putting your feet,' he warned her. 'Even in boots you can come a cropper.'

They stood still for a moment while she regained her breath and looked around her. The wet woods gleamed with the russets and golds of autumn, and the water—higher than usual, Nick told her, because of all the rain—was Mediterranean-blue beneath a cloudless sky.

'It looks very inviting,' she observed as they moved on.

'Exhilarating is more the word,' he corrected ruefully. 'Finn and I used to swim here a lot as boys, and believe me it's *cold*—even in summer.'

'Finn...' she mused. 'It's an unusual name.'

'He's an unusual man. An intelligent, multi-talented Swede who could have been anything he chose. He can speak several languages, he's an excellent musician and he qualified as a doctor before he decided to join me in business. His family belonged originally to Maine's Swedish colony before they moved down to Boston.'

'I gather you and he virtually grew up together?'

'We were and still are like brothers. The Andersons, as well as being our neighbours, were good friends, and we always spent our vacations together. In those days they rented a rather tumbledown cabin on the far side of the creek, though Finn usually stayed in ours.'

He smiled reminiscently. 'Despite her fear of bears, my mother used to allow us to bed down on the porch—we thought it was more adventurous than sleeping indoors...'

But all at once Raine didn't want to hear. To know more about his boyhood would only serve to bring him that much closer, to deepen her feelings, when what she needed to do was tear herself free from the emotional bonds that were already binding her to him.

'And instead of making us eat with the others, she used to let us cook sausages and beans over our own campfire... When my mother died, Inga Anderson took me under her wing...'

'How old were you then?'

'Eleven. An awkward, inarticulate age. But Inga seemed to know how I felt. Without making a fuss, she gave me all the comfort I needed and as much love as she gave her own children.'

'Is she—?' Raine began.

Face clouding, Nick shook his head. 'She and her husband Nils died in an accident on the freeway about eighteen months ago.'

It was obvious he still felt their loss.

Before she could express any sympathy, however, he was going on, 'Finn went through a rough patch, but he...' The sound of a plane's engine drowned his words.

They both looked up. The white aircraft with its orange

and blue markings was almost overhead, flying low, heading across the lake.

Raising an arm, Nick waved.

The squared-off wings dipped in answer.

'Talk of the devil,' he said with a grin.

'That's Finn?'

'That's Finn.'

'How did he know it was you?'

'I left a message at the office, telling him I was planning to bring you up here.'

'Oh…'

'He's taking a couple of construction engineers over to the camp at Loon Lake,' Nick went on as the small plane disappeared into the distance. 'At a guess he'll spend the night there and do the return trip tomorrow. There's a possibility he'll stop in to see us on his way back.'

Raine bit her lip. With so much on her mind she was hardly in the mood for company.

'You don't appear to be very pleased at the prospect,' Nick remarked. When she stayed silent, he pressed, 'I rather thought you liked Finn?'

'I do.' And it was the truth. She had taken to the quiet, pleasantly spoken man on sight. 'So does Margo,' she added with a slight smile.

'I fancy the attraction is mutual,' Nick observed. 'So when we get back to England we may be seeing more of him.'

'I'm not sure he's really Margo's type.' Raine spoke her thoughts aloud.

'What is Margo's type?'

'She needs a very strong character—a man she can respect and who's capable of being dominant. But often she's attracted to the quiet, sensitive sort, like Finn.'

Nick raised an eyebrow, but said nothing.

'Basically she has a kind, sunny nature, but a *positive* personality that tends to overwhelm the kind of men she falls for, and then she's disappointed when they can't stand up to her.'

Seeing Nick's wry expression, Raine asked, 'You think I'm misjudging her?'

'I think you're misjudging Finn. He may be sensitive, but he's not soft in any way. In fact he's a hell of a lot tougher than he looks. If I had my back to the wall, either figuratively or literally, there's no man I'd rather have by my side...'

In the light of those remarks Raine found herself hoping that Nick was right about the attraction between Margo and Finn being mutual.

'What kind of woman does Finn go for?' she asked curiously.

'Margo might well fit the bill. I know he hasn't much time for the empty-headed clinging-vine sort. He once told me that if he married, he'd like a woman who would stand by his side and fight if the going got tough. All the same, Finn's protective, and he has the capacity to love deeply and lastingly...'

Oh, lucky, lucky Margo, Raine thought, and tried not to let her own bitterness swamp her.

'He also has a nice sense of humour. I remember once when we were boys and a rather staid family friend came on vacation with us...'

For the remainder of the walk Nick talked about Finn, making her laugh despite the pain that burnt inside like acid.

When they got back Nick cooked delicious buckwheat pancakes for lunch, and doused them in maple syrup.

Despite her enormous breakfast, Raine managed two, and she wondered a shade bleakly if the walk had given her an appetite or if she was merely comfort-eating, using food as a substitute for happiness.

Their coffee finished, Nick made up the stove before querying, 'Would you like to take the canoe and have a trip round the lake? Or if you prefer, and you've had enough fresh air for one day, we could stay indoors and play games?'

On one of the bookcase shelves, beside a large first aid box, there was a chess set, a crib board and some cards and various other games.

However, his sly glance at the bed had made it amply clear what kind of games he had in mind, and she said hastily, 'Oh, a trip round the lake.'

His smile was sardonic. 'A prompt, if unflattering answer.'

'It seems a shame to waste the sunshine.' She managed to keep her voice level.

'Perhaps it does.' A glint in his eye, he added reflectively, 'The nights are long at this time of the year.'

On her previous visit, Nick had taught Raine how to balance the canoe and wield one of the short broad-bladed paddles, and after a trial run close to the shore, it soon came back to her.

She wore a knitted hat pulled well down over her ears, but he was bareheaded in the sunshine. He sat in front of her and she found herself wanting to touch the back of his neck, to run her fingers through the thick tow-coloured hair that curled slightly into his nape…

'Ready to start?' he queried, glancing over his shoulder.

'Yes, I'm ready,' she answered quickly, and, feeling a betraying warmth creeping into her cheeks, was glad when he turned his gaze to the front.

Steering to avoid the rougher section, where the brown creek emptied itself into the blue lake, Nick remarked with a chuckle, 'Finn and I used to take it in turns to ride a home-made raft the length of the creek. Standing…'

'Standing?' she echoed incredulously.

'It didn't count as a proper run unless you did. After Owl Pond there's a straight stretch, then a U-bend before the rapids. An old wooden footbridge used to span the creek just above the bend, and the real skill—apart from shooting the rapids—was in ducking low enough to clear it without losing your balance.

'I wouldn't care to try it at the moment,' he added. 'Even at low water the rapids can be tricky. With all this rain there'll be a raging torrent coming down...'

But out on the mirror-calm lake it was peaceful enough. The rhythmic dip of the paddle, the chuckle of the water and the curtsying motion of the light craft were oddly soothing, and Raine would have thoroughly enjoyed the afternoon if she hadn't been made tense and on edge by the thought of the approaching night.

She wanted him... Oh, how she wanted him! But while her body welcomed his touch ecstatically her mind found it intolerable, and the ensuing conflict threatened to tear her apart and destroy her.

And each time it would get worse. She would want him just a little bit more, slip just a little bit more into his power, until she was unable to leave him. Then, when his obsession was cured and he grew tired of her...

Nick glanced back over his shoulder.

Raine bit her lip and, afraid he would pick up her agitation, as he so often picked up what she was thinking and feeling, tried to calm herself.

But still the panicky thoughts jostled through her head. She *had* to get away! Yet leaving on foot was out of the question. She would have to be suicidal to attempt it. And, though desperate, she wasn't suicidal...

If only she could get her hands on the keys to the Cherokee...

Eyes unseeing, thoughts busy, she paddled mechanically until the bottom of the canoe grating against the smooth stony bed of the shallows, startled her.

Midnight-blue eyes on her face, Nick asked, 'Something bothering you?'

'No, no...'

'You look to be in a mental turmoil.'

Oh, but he was too clever by half.

Raine was naturally truthful, lies didn't come easily to her, and she was painfully aware that she sounded ill at ease as she seized on what he'd told her earlier. 'I—I was just thinking of you and Finn rafting down the creek. Surely it must have been terribly dangerous?'.

He seemed to accept her explanation, however, answering casually, 'Not really. We only attempted it when the conditions were right.'

Pushing himself up, he jumped out of the light craft with the cat-like agility that seemed almost disconcerting in so big a man and, a foot steadying the prow, held out his hand. Reluctantly she took it, and was hauled up to step out into an inch or so of lapping wavelets.

Looking back, she saw a gossamer mist was beginning to form on the lake; the sun had gone and the sky, flaming orange and gold in the west, was flecked with purple cloud. Wings whirring, honking loudly, a skein of geese flew in V-formation low over the water.

Beneath the trees a blue dusk was creeping out of hiding, and the pungent scent of woodsmoke hung on the hazy air. It was almost evening. Soon it would be night.

She shivered a little, and in silence helped him carry the canoe the short distance to the cabin and restow it.

Alongside the veranda was an old tree stump that was used as a chopping block. While Raine went and took off her outdoor things Nick fetched a pile of dry logs and, having stripped off his jacket and hung it over the veranda rail, began to split them.

Hearing the strokes of the heavy axe ringing out in the stillness, she was suddenly galvanised into action. While he was occupied this was her chance to look for the keys to the Cherokee.

Heart racing, feeling guilty as a thief, she searched his belongings, going through his trouser and coat pockets with care, but finding only his wallet, a sealed envelope, a folded handkerchief, a penknife, a comb, his house keys and a handful of dollars, dimes, quarters and nickels.

He must be carrying the car keys on him.

Biting back her disappointment, knowing she mustn't appear upset when he came in, she made an effort to calm herself while she lit the gas-lights and boiled water for a pot of coffee.

By the time Nick had finished his task and carried in a plentiful supply of split logs, the gathering clouds were making it practically dark outside, and there was a spit of rain on the windows.

Looking up from the meal she had started to prepare, Raine saw that there were several woodchips in his thick fair hair and a fine sheen of perspiration on his hard-boned face.

'There's some coffee ready,' she said.

'Keep it hot,' he suggested briefly. 'I'll shower off first.'

Hanging his black leather jacket on one of the hooks, he disappeared into the bathroom.

It was, she realised with sudden hope, the jacket he'd worn the previous evening. Holding her breath, she hurried over to feel in the pockets, and heard the rattle of the keys before her eager fingers touched them.

Her luck seemed to be in. Along with the keys came an unexpected bonus—her wallet containing her driving licence and credit cards.

Thrusting it into the pocket of her trousers with desperate haste, she then pulled on a pair of flat shoes and an anorak, and, snatching up her mud-stained handbag, made for the door, closing it behind her with care and wincing when the latch clicked loudly in the silence.

Heart racing, she crept down the veranda steps and pocked her way over the muddy ground. A breeze had sprung up, blowing a tendril of hair against her cheek and ruffling her half-fringe, and it had started to rain in earnest.

She felt a qualm or two about starting out in the dark, but she didn't dare wait until morning. There might not be another chance.

The Cherokee's lights were good, and as soon as she'd

crossed the creek and found her way back to the logging road the worst would be over, she told herself stoutly.

But suppose there was nothing to indicate in which direction Bangor lay?

Mentally squaring her shoulders, Raine decided that it was no use worrying ahead; she would jump that hurdle when she came to it.

Nervousness making her fumble, she dropped the keys in the mud, wasting precious seconds searching for them. As soon as she had them safe once more, she found the right one and opened the car door. Climbing behind the wheel, she pulled the door to carefully, afraid to bang it, and, hands shaking, fitted the key into the ignition.

The engine sprang into life immediately. She was just breathing a sigh of relief when the door swung open again and Nick stood there, bare to the waist, a towel slung around his neck. 'Thinking of going somewhere?' he asked crisply.

Shock made her a split second too slow. Just as she tried to press the accelerator he switched off the engine and removed the keys in one swift movement. The next moment she was hauled out, none too gently, and propelled back the way she'd come, his fingers biting painfully into the soft flesh of her upper arm.

Blinking a little in the light, she watched apprehensively as he closed the heavy door with a decisive thud and pushed home the bolt.

When he turned to face her, she saw he was livid. With a kind of raging calm, he asked, 'How the *hell* did you think you were going to find your way in the dark?'

'*You* did,' she pointed out defiantly.

'I'm familiar with the backwoods. You're not.'

As he advanced towards her she had to summon every ounce of courage not to back away, and somehow she managed to stand her ground, even when he loomed over her.

Pulling off her anorak, he tossed that and her bag aside,

demanding, 'Have you the *faintest* idea of the risks you were running?'

'Getting lost was preferable to staying here.'

'You silly little fool!' he snarled. 'The weather's deteriorating, and if you'd got bogged down or hopelessly lost, the only other people you'd have been remotely likely to encounter would have been hunters or backpackers on the Allagash trip. Most, no doubt, are decent men, but you *might* have met the sort who would consider a lone woman fair game.'

Then his anger and exasperation boiled over. 'I've a damned good mind to turn you over my knee and teach you a lesson you won't forget in a hurry.'

Terrified of his fury, of the violence she'd aroused, she played the only card she'd got. 'Then why don't you?' she cried scornfully. 'You're a big strong man. I can't stop you.'

'Exactly!' His eyes blazed. 'And you'd have had even less chance of stopping a group of half-drunken hunters.'

Her lip curled contemptuously. 'So I should think myself lucky to be with a man who gets his kicks from telling me what *might* have happened to me?'

'If we're talking about kicks perhaps I should *show* you what might have happened to you.'

She was wearing a checked woollen shirt, and, taking hold of the lapels, he wrenched them apart, ripping the buttons from the buttonholes and tearing the fabric.

At her cry of outrage, he said with icy determination, 'Unless you want me to rip the rest of your clothes from your back, you'd better take them off. And fast.'

'I hate you!' she spat at him while, hands shaking, she obeyed his command.

He stripped off the rest of her clothes and, as soon as she was naked, hooked her feet from under her, sending her sprawling on the rug. He followed her down, leaving her in no doubt that he really did mean to take her brutally, to prove a point and to teach her an object lesson.

Her breathing was quick and harsh, and her pulse seemed to slam through her veins. But she made no attempt to struggle. She wouldn't fight him—wouldn't let him have the satisfaction of subduing her.

Looking at her set face, he said softly, 'No, perhaps not. Rather than just taking you, I think I'll get a great deal more pleasure from making you respond when you so obviously don't want to.'

Grasping her chin in one hand, he forced her to meet his eyes. Seeing the defiance in her dark-pupiled green stare, he smiled mirthlessly. 'Well, my darling wife, shall we see how long it will take to set you alight?'

Lips pressed together, she said nothing.

His tongue-tip traced the outline of her mouth, then moved across her lips, parting them to stroke the sensitive inner skin.

She gave a throaty gasp, and he began to kiss her lightly, sensuously. Feeling her lips quiver betrayingly beneath his, he whispered, 'I don't think it will take too long.'

He slid a hand beneath her back and arched her towards him, using his fingers and his mouth and his voice to pleasure her until, lost and on fire for him, she signalled her surrender by turning her face into his tanned throat.

Moving with maddening slowness, he began to make love to her—a leisurely prolonged building of sensation until she was poised on the brink.

But, instead of going on to give her the satisfaction she craved, he lifted himself away a little and, spreading his hands over the cradle of her hips, began to move them in a rocking motion.

She tried to stiffen, but he was in control, making her move as he wanted her to move, generating a liquid heat, building an almost unbearable core of tension inside her with knowledge and consummate skill.

His lovemaking was as inventive as it was erotic, and finally her whole body jerked and quivered in a wild explosion of ecstasy.

As though to prove his dominance once and for all, he took her to the heights repeatedly, until she was limp and mindless, her entire being melted by the white-hot heat of passion.

Then, leaving her lying there, eyes closed, drained of all emotion, he got up and pulled on some clothes.

A short while later she heard him rattling pots and pans as he took over the cooking of their belated meal.

The heat from the stove was no compensation for the warmth of his body and she shivered, gathering up her clothes and making her way to the bathroom, staggering a little like someone inebriated.

She hated both him and herself with a fierce and bitter hatred. Remembering her declaration that if he was up to his neck in quicksand she wouldn't lift a finger to help, that she'd stand and cheer while he went under, she told herself that though she might not have meant it *then*, she certainly meant it *now*.

She showered and, her resentment growing, deliberately dressed in the things she had worn earlier, though the shirt gaped open, exposing her low-cut bra and the curves of her breasts.

Let him feel ashamed of the way he had treated her.

But if he felt any shame he certainly didn't show it. When she emerged from the bathroom he looked up and, allowing his gaze to travel slowly over her from head to toe, said with cool arrogance, 'Come here.'

She knew she should refuse such a peremptory demand, make some kind of a stand for independence, but, though her expression was mutinous, somehow her legs carried her across the few feet of space.

He had the air of a conqueror when, his hard face triumphant, he bent to touch his lips to hers.

Jerking away, she demanded bitterly, '*Another* kiss of peace?'

'*You* broke the truce,' he pointed out. 'But hopefully, now the war's over, *this* peace will be longer lasting.'

Raine looked at him with angry, resentful eyes. If he thought the war was over he was wrong! All he'd won was a battle.

CHAPTER TEN

THOUGH it rained heavily during the early part of the night, towards dawn it cleared, and Nick opened the curtains to another bright sunshiny day.

'Ideal for a ride to Saskis Pond,' he remarked. 'When we've had breakfast I'll pack the kind of picnic lunch Finn and I used to take.'

'Speaking of Finn, didn't you say he might call?'

'He probably won't leave Loon Lake until after lunch, so if we get an early start we should be home in plenty of time.'

When they'd eaten, and the picnic was ready, Nick suggested, 'If you want to drive round to the Doodys' with me, we could start from there.'

'Well, I...' Her eyes strayed to the marks on his hard cheek.

'Ah!' Realising the source of her discomfort, he fingered the scratches.

She flushed. 'What will they *think*?'

His eyes held a teasing gleam. 'When I tell them we're up here on honeymoon, they'll think I have a very passionate wife.'

He watched her colour deepen and, making no effort to hide his amusement, went on, 'Ah, well, if you're too shy to come, I'll leave the car there and ride back.' Pulling on his coat, he went to the door.

Unsettled and jumpy, she followed him through the porch and out onto the veranda.

Taking the steps two at a time, he slid behind the Cherokee's wheel. 'I'll be back in about an hour,' he called. The door slammed and he was off.

Raine watched until the four-wheel-drive went out of sight amongst the trees, then, unwilling to stay indoors, she pulled on an anorak and changed her shoes for a pair of boots before walking down to the water's edge.

Off to the right a streak of red caught her eye, and she saw a one-man canoe being paddled along parallel to the shore.

On an impulse she hailed the occupant.

'Hi there!' he replied cheerfully, and paddled towards her until she heard the light craft grate on the stony bottom.

He was young, little more than eighteen or nineteen, and his fair face was pleasantly open. 'You don't sound as though you come from the States,' he remarked.

'I'm English,' she admitted.

'Staying in these parts?'

She waved a hand. 'At the cabin. What about you?'

'Been on my second Allagash trip. Fantastic!' He sighed. 'Unfortunately this is the last day. In less than an hour I'll be on my way back to Augusta.'

'Presumably not by canoe?' Raine asked lightly, while her heart leapt with sudden excitement.

'I've a pick-up truck parked about a mile away—just off one of the logging roads. I follow the inlet—' he pointed beyond the creek to a narrow curving arm of the lake '—to the end, then all it takes is a short portage.

'Well, I must get on.' As he began to ease the canoe back into deeper water he added with an engaging grin, 'I'm picking my girlfriend up in Bangor, and there'll be the devil to pay if I'm late.'

'Wait! Please, wait,' Raine begged.

Looking startled by the sudden urgency in her voice, he paused, water dripping from the end of his paddle. 'Something wrong?'

'Yes, I...I *desperately* need to get back to Bangor straight away. Please can you take me?'

'Well... I suppose so... But surely you have some transport?'

Raine was about to shake her head when he added, 'I caught sight of a big four-wheel-drive on the track only a minute or two ago.'

'That's my...' Realising she couldn't tell him the truth, she broke off. Then, her mind working like lightning, she went on, 'My American cousin. He's gone to visit some friends. Letting him bring me up here was a ghastly mistake, and now to avoid a scene I want to get away before he comes back.'

The canoeist looked uncomfortable, and, seeing his gaze fixed on her left hand, where her rings had flashed in the sun, she added hastily, 'You see, I'm married, and I thought I could trust him. But as soon as we got here I discovered he had no intention of keeping things platonic.'

'Have you only just arrived?'

Taking a chance, she lied, 'Yes... We managed a very early start this morning.'

Plainly reluctant to get involved, the canoeist hesitated.

'Oh, *please*,' she begged.

'Well, OK... But you'll have to make your own way to the pick-up. It's less than a mile if you go direct through the woods...' He pointed. 'There's a narrow trail starts just behind the cabin. It leads to a footbridge that spans the creek above the bend.'

That must be the old footbridge Nick had talked about, Raine thought.

'Once across that, head for a spur of rock with a single pine growing on it. The pick-up is parked in the lee of it... Oh, and wear something bright orange if you can; it's the hunting season.'

Pulling away from the shore, he began to paddle. 'So long as you don't waste any time, you should easily be there before me. If you're not waiting by the truck, I'll presume you've changed your mind...'

Stumbling in her haste, Raine turned and headed back

to the porch, where she pulled on one of the orange plastic waistcoats and a matching woollen hat.

Though the track was littered with debris from the recent storm, it was comparatively easy to follow, and, afraid of the canoeist leaving without her, Raine hurried over the rough rocky ground as fast as she dared.

She heard the sound of the creek before she reached it, and she spurred herself on with the thought that the footbridge lay just ahead.

But when she finally emerged from the trees she saw with a shock that the turbulent brown water had carried away some of the old rotting timbers. Part of the handrail had gone, and on the far side there was a jagged two-foot gap. What was left of the planking was awash.

But she *couldn't* turn back now.

Just as she reached the bridge she heard a warning shout above the noise of the water. Ignoring it, she clung to the handrail and began to inch her way across.

She was about a third of the way over when there was a dull crack and the whole structure tilted at a crazy angle.

In the split second before she fell, as though in slow motion, she saw Nick wheel his horse and gallop away.

But he wouldn't leave her. He *wouldn't...*

The shock of the cold water closing over her and the ferocity of its onslaught should have paralysed her wits. Instead she found her brain oddly clear and lucid as she was swept into the bend—the bed of the creek at this point was blessedly free of boulders.

Weighted down by her clothes and boots, it was impossible to swim, and she had to fight hard just to keep her head above water.

Apart from a few stunted trees trying to find a foothold in the stony soil, the surrounding area was open, and as she was carried along by the force of the water Raine caught a fleeting glimpse of a horse at full stretch, the rider crouched low on its neck.

Suddenly written in her mind in letters of fire was Nick's

description of the creek—'there's a straight stretch, then a U-bend before the rapids'—and she knew *why* he had ridden away. The water was flowing much too fast for him to have any chance of reaching her, so he was racing across the narrow neck of the U to try to get ahead and intercept her before she was swept to her death down the rapids.

The certainty that Nick was trying to save her gave her fresh heart, and she did her best to battle against the powerful current that, following the angle of the bend, was tending to sweep her towards the far bank.

'Raine!'

A shout drew her attention, and she saw that Nick was ahead and to her right. Stripped to the waist, he was waiting, coolly judging his moment. Just before she drew level, he plunged into the creek.

A moment later one strong arm grasped her and held her tightly while, swimming diagonally, using the water rather than trying to fight it, he waited for the current to sweep them into the opposite bank.

By the time they were close enough they had been carried round the bend and were at the top of the rapids, with the water tumbling and boiling between huge boulders. Here the bank was higher and extremely hazardous, with sharp edges of jutting rock.

As they were swept along he caught hold of the overhanging branch of a small lopsided fir tree and hung on, struggling to find some kind of foothold, shielding her body with his own as the surging water tried to batter them against the rocks.

Making a superhuman effort, he lifted Raine with his free arm until she was almost clear of the water, but, before he could brace himself to push, a sudden surge dashed him against a jagged spur of rock.

For a second or two she hung there, without the necessary strength to pull herself up the bank. As though part of her mind stood aloof, detached, above the noise of the water she heard the sharp cry of some bird and the drone of a plane low overhead.

'Move, damn you!' Nick's command cracked like a whip. 'If you slip back I may not be able to lift you again.'

Galvanised into action, she grasped at a projecting piece of rock and managed to haul herself to safety, expecting Nick to follow.

When he didn't, she turned to see why.

He was still holding onto the branch with his right hand, but his left arm was hanging useless.

As she went down on her knees the force of the water knocked him sideways, and she cried out in shock as his head hit the rock with sickening force.

Somehow he kept his hold, but his face was grey, his eyes closed, and there was blood on his temple which reappeared every time the surging water washed it away.

While she stared in horror the fingers holding the branch began to lose their grip.

Falling flat on her stomach, she leaned over and fastened both hands tightly around his wrist, trying to dig her toes in as his weight and the pull of the water threatened to drag her back.

He opened glazed eyes. 'Let go, you little fool.' His voice was thick, the words slurred. 'You'll never be able to get me out… You're just risking your own life… Leave me…'

But just as she had known instinctively that he wouldn't leave her, she knew that she couldn't leave him. She would sooner die with him than live without him.

No, she would sooner they both lived!

Gathering herself, she called for help as loudly as she could, though common sense told her they had been carried so far downstream that the canoeist would be out of earshot.

When she could call no more she held on with every ounce of her failing strength, teeth clenched, refusing to give up hope, while her fingers whitened and her arms felt as if they were being torn from their sockets.

'Hang on!'

She had drifted into a kind of stupor when the shout roused her. *Had* there really been a shout? she wondered dazedly. Or was she starting to hallucinate?

'Hang on!' It came again, producing a new surge of hope which gave her fresh strength.

A moment or two later a man threw himself down beside her and, with a longer reach, grasped Nick's arm just above the elbow. Calmly, he announced, 'I've got him. You can let go now.'

She had to make an effort to release her grip, which seemed to have frozen in place.

Lifting a head which lolled a little, Nick muttered, 'Finn?'

'In person, old son,' Finn said briskly. Then, to Raine, 'There's some rope. Double it, slip it under my arms, pass the ends through the loop to make a noose and, leaving some slack, tie both ends securely round the tree trunk.'

Picking up the small coil of climbing rope he'd dropped she followed his instructions as swiftly as her stiff fingers would allow.

'What now?'

'Hold onto Nick again…'

Once more both her hands closed over Nick's lean wrist The instant Finn was satisfied that her grip was secure, he relinquished his own and pulled the noose into position.

'I don't know whether he's conscious enough to be able to do much, so as soon as I can take some of his weight pull for all you're worth.'

Leaning back on the rope, bracing his feet against the rocky bank as though he was abseiling, Finn went into the creek downstream of Nick.

With amazing strength for such a slimly built man, he began to heave Nick's bulk clear of the surging water while

Raine, remembering the school tug of war team, used all her weight to pull.

Though obviously only half conscious, as soon as his bare feet were able to find a purchase on the rock, Nick fought to help himself.

A few seconds later both men were safe on the bank and, water streaming from his clothes, Finn was kneeling, checking Nick's injuries.

Terrified by his greyish pallor, she whispered, 'How is he?'

Glancing up, Finn said reassuringly, 'Could be worse. A blow to the head, which has dazed him, and a dislocated shoulder.' He touched the extensive lacerations on the bare chest. 'Possibly some cracked ribs… But he's a tough nut.'

Nick groaned, and muttering, 'Thanks,' sat up.

His face was still ashen and the blood continued to ooze from the nasty gash on his temple, but he seemed to be more or less conscious now.

Focusing on Raine, as though with difficulty, he asked thickly, urgently, 'Are *you* all right?'

'I'm fine,' she assured him, the relief of having him out of danger so great that she could give no expression to it.

Finn turned his attention to Raine, taking her almost unnatural composure, her look of cold, white-faced exhaustion. 'Sure?' he asked, untying the rope and coiling it neatly and expertly.

'Quite sure.'

'Come on then, old son.' Lending a hand to haul the other man to his feet, Finn settled Nick's good arm around his shoulders. 'What we need to do is get moving before hypothermia sets in.'

'We're on the wrong side of the creek,' Raine remarked as, a shade unsteadily, they began to make their way over the rough ground. 'I mean, we can't go back over the footbridge…'

Finn shook his head. 'No need. Luckily the plane's quite close…'

Yes, she vaguely recalled hearing a plane…

'I was circling to come down on the lake when I spotted you—thank heavens those orange vests are so visible, and thank the Lord I decided to come back early—and I landed on the road instead.'

A minute or so later the small white plane with its orange and blue markings came into view. In the middle of the muddy road and slightly slewed, its door still open, it bore silent witness to Finn's desperate urgency.

When Raine, outwardly still and calm, had climbed into the rear, he helped Nick into the co-pilot's seat and said cheerfully, 'We'll be back in a few minutes.'

By the time they had touched down on the lake and struggled to the cabin reaction had set in, and she was shaking like a leaf.

Dropping the grip he'd brought from the plane, Finn splashed brandy into three glasses and, having handed her one, said, 'Drink that, then jump into a hot bath. Nick and I will towel ourselves down and get changed in front of the stove.'

When she emerged from the bathroom some fifteen minutes later both men were dressed, though Nick was still shirtless, and there was a pot of coffee on the stove.

Marvelling at his powers of recuperation, she saw his face had lost the greyish pallor that had frightened her so much, and, though there were lines of pain drawn around his mouth, his eyes were once more bright and alert.

She wanted to put her arms round him and hold him close, to sob out her relief against his heart, but he was looking at her as though she was a stranger.

'Feeling better now?' Finn asked.

'Much better.' She smiled at the slim, dark-haired man whose thin face held a quiet, indomitable strength, and wondered how she could ever have suspected him of being weak.

The first aid box at his elbow, he had started to apply

antiseptic to the gash on Nick's temple. 'If you don't have this stitched it will probably leave a scar,' he observed.

'I'm not planning to enter any beauty contests,' Nick answered drily.

Finn grinned. 'Just as well, with an ugly mug like yours.'

He finished his ministrations and covered the wound with a pad held in place by a strip of sticking-plaster, before turning his attention to the bruised and lacerated ribs.

Nick grunted as he pressed them, but denied that there was any need to strap them up.

'That shoulder needs setting,' Finn remarked. 'Shall I fly you back to Bangor?'

'You used to be able to set a shoulder,' Nick suggested.

Finn hesitated, frowning.

'Can I help?' Raine asked.

Meeting her steady gaze, Finn said, 'Thank the Lord you're not squeamish.'

Lifting Nick's left arm until it was parallel with his shoulder, he instructed her. 'What I want you to do is keep it steady, and at this height.'

While she held the arm at the required angle Finn went to stand behind Nick with the palm of his hand pressed against the bare muscular shoulder, and, taking hold of him in what looked like a half-nelson, he gave a sudden jerk.

Raine heard the sharp crack as the bone settled back into place, and winced.

Nick didn't utter a sound, though the pain had made a fine beading of perspiration spring out on his brow and upper lip.

With a fierce surge of almost maternal love and tenderness she wanted to wipe it away, to kiss the tautness from around his mouth.

A blue and green lumberjack-type shirt was hanging over a chair. Picking it up, she began to help him on with it. Unable to meet his eyes, afraid he would read what was in hers, she kept her head bent and watched her own fingers fastening the buttons with care.

When she had finished he tucked it into his trousers one-handed while Finn folded a square of cotton material from the first aid box to make a sling.

When it was neatly in place, he said to his patient, 'Now, take the weight off your feet and try to get comfortable.' Then, with a conspiratorial wink at Raine, 'This might be the only chance I ever get to boss him about.'

Nick lowered himself into one of the armchairs with a grunt and complained, 'I was a damned sight more comfortable standing up.'

'Ungrateful swine,' Finn said mildly, and shook a couple of white tablets into his hand. 'You'll need painkillers for the next day or so. I suggest that when these have had time to take effect, you have a lie down. Both of you.' He smiled at Raine. 'In the meantime I'll pour some coffee, and you can tell me exactly what happened.'

Her throat closed up tight. She swallowed hard and said, 'I haven't even thanked you yet…'

'No thanks are necessary.'

'You saved Nick's life.'

'No, *you* saved Nick's life. If you hadn't hung on to him like you did, he would have been a goner before I could have reached him. It was a very courageous thing to do.'

'But I could never have managed to get him out. You were absolutely marvellous…'

'God give me strength!' Nick muttered. Then went on, '*I'm* the one who should be thanking both of *you*! And I will, as soon as you've finished forming a mutual admiration society.'

The tension burst in a bubble of laughter.

When they'd sobered, Raine looked up and found Nick's eyes fixed on her. Quickly she shook her head. 'If it hadn't been for you *I* would have died.' Remembering the thundering force of the water, she shuddered.

'And don't thank me,' Finn said. 'I was merely evening the score. Remember the time I went through the ice...?'

'You were only fourteen.'

'Still counts.'

As they sat around drinking the coffee Finn had poured he asked plaintively, 'So isn't anyone going to tell me how it happened?'

'We'd planned a ride to Saskis Pond.' It was Nick who answered, his voice smooth and controlled. 'So I'd driven over to the Doodys' to borrow a couple of horses.

'Raine had gone for a walk, and, riding back through the woods, I spotted her about to try and cross the old footbridge. It's been half-rotten for years. I called out to her...'

Did he really think she'd been just taking a walk? No, surely not. Bearing in mind how she'd carried on in spite of his warning, he must have guessed at least part of the truth.

'But it was too late...' Briefly and unemotionally he filled in the rest, ending crisply, 'And now it's about time somebody rounded up Lisbet's horses.'

Finn rose to his feet and said good-naturedly, 'I can take a hint. Though I might point out that if you'd had the sense to do what most honeymooners do—i.e. stay in bed—it wouldn't have been necessary.'

He ducked, and the cushion Nick threw at him sailed over his head.

'Despite that disgusting display of fitness, you won't be doing any riding for a while, so I'll return the horses and bring the Cherokee back.' He added seriously, 'There might be some delayed shock, so while I'm gone you two rest. Doctor's orders.'

When the door had closed behind him, Nick sat staring into the flames, the expression on his face withdrawn, sombre, while the silence lengthened and tension stretched between them like fine steel wires.

When she could bear it no longer, Raine jumped to her feet and said hoarsely, inadequately, 'Nick, I'm sorry.'

'For what?' He didn't even look at her.

'It was my stupidity that almost cost you your life.'

'*Both* our lives,' he said harshly. 'Dear God, you must have been desperate to have gone onto that bridge. It was suicidal...' He lifted his head, and she saw the dark blue eyes grow almost black.

'No!' she denied sharply. 'That was never the intention. I was trying to get across. You see...' She told him about the canoeist and, watching his expression, added hastily, 'He was young and pleasant. He had a girlfriend in Bangor...'

'But if he'd been the Boston Strangler you'd still have gone with him,' Nick said heavily. 'You really must hate and detest me to take such risks.'

No, she didn't hate him. She'd *wanted* to hate him, *tried* to hate him. But love had always proved stronger, and she'd feared that love more than she'd feared him. Feared it would destroy her and leave only a burnt-out shell.

But the closeness of death had made her realise how precious life was—too precious to waste a minute of it in futile regrets for what was past, or fear of what was to come.

'No, Nick, I—'

His mouth tight, he shook his head, and said with black bitterness, 'You've told me so plenty of times. I just haven't wanted to believe it.'

'But I *don't* hate you—'

'There's no need to deny it now, just because you think I saved your life. After all, it wouldn't have been in danger if it hadn't been for me.'

Physically and emotionally drained, she staggered a little and pressed waxy fingers to her forehead. 'If you'd only *listen*—'

'You're about out on your feet,' he interrupted curtly. 'It's time you were getting that rest Finn mentioned.'

'Perhaps it's time we *both* were,' she said without moving, making it clear that she had no intention of going alone.

Stiffly, grimacing a little, he got to his feet and said, 'Very well. You take that bed—it'll be warmer. I'll use the bedroom.'

Shocked, she watched him walk away and close the bedroom door after him. Had he decided to use the spare room because he was angry with her? Or was it that he didn't want her to see that he was in pain?

Knowing it was more likely to be the latter, she felt rebuffed and miserable.

But it was her own fault. She could hear herself telling him bitterly, "You once said that all you wanted from me was the use of my body, and that's all you'll ever get! Not comfort or concern if you're injured or ill, not help and support when you're tired and you need a shoulder to lean on, not compassion—"

Snapping off the painful memory like a dry twig, she fought the urge to follow him and tell him she hadn't meant it. Clearly, at the moment, he didn't want her near him, nor did he want to hear anything she had to say.

With so much burning in her mind Raine didn't expect to sleep, but, within seconds of taking off her blouse and skirt and climbing into bed, she went out like a light.

She awakened to find that Finn had returned. He and Nick were sitting by the stove talking in undertones while they ate the picnic Nick had prepared that morning.

The bedside clock showed that it was early afternoon; she'd slept for over two hours. Feeling suddenly ravenous, she pulled on her clothes and went to join them.

Both men glanced up at her approach, and something in their expressions made her heart stand still and then begin to hammer with alarm.

Nick's face was set and stony, while Finn's wore a look of dismay and perplexity.

A pricking in her thumbs warned her to play it cool.

Nick was sitting on the settee, and, careful not to jolt him, she took a seat by his side. There were several drink cans in front of him, and the food, still in its wrappers, was spread out on the small coffee-table.

'May I?' Raine helped herself to a thick round slice of the brown malted fruit bread that came in a tin. She was reaching for a chunk of ham when Finn half rose. 'Shall I get you a fork?'

'It's supposed to be a picnic, isn't it?' she asked lightly.

'Sure is,' he agreed.

'Then I'll eat with my fingers the same as everyone else.'

There was an awkward silence before Finn asked, 'Had a good rest?'

'I've been sound asleep for ages... Did you have any trouble finding Mrs Doody's horses?'

'None at all. I told her about the accident and she sends her commiserations. Says to go over for a meal one day soon and—' Finn broke off abruptly.

Knowing *something* was wrong, Raine took a deep breath. 'That's very nice of her,' she said evenly, and then to Nick, 'Perhaps when your shoulder is better we could—'

'We won't be staying,' he told her brusquely. 'At least *you* won't.'

CHAPTER ELEVEN

A GIANT fist seemed to close around her heart. So that was it. He had decided to let her go. And she knew with great certainty that if she went everything they had shared—the humour, the passion, the stimulating companionship—would all be lost, and their brief marriage would be over.

But why was he letting her go? Not because he didn't want her any longer, she was sure, but because he was finally convinced she hated him.

Shaking her head, she began, 'Nick, I—'

'If you'll excuse me a minute.' Finn rose to his feet. 'I just want to take a look at the weather.'

When the door had closed behind the other man, Nick went on, his eyes bleak, 'As soon as you've had something to eat and packed your things, Finn will take you back to Bangor and see you on a plane for Boston.'

Briefly she wondered how much Finn knew. Not the whole truth; she would stake her life on that. He would be merely carrying out instructions. Instructions that had clearly surprised and dismayed him.

Keeping her voice steady with an effort, she said, 'That's very kind of him. But what about you?'

'I'll stay on for a day or so and drive back when my shoulder's up to it... Of course, if you'd prefer it, Finn's happy to travel all the way to Boston with you.'

That gave her the opening she needed. Knowing now how she was going to play it, she asked in dulcet tones, 'Was that *his* suggestion or *yours*?'

Casting her a rapier-sharp glance, Nick answered briefly, 'Mine.'

'Good!' Her green eyes flashed. 'Then as your wife I can tell you exactly what I think of it, and of you. It's the most insulting suggestion I've ever heard! And you are a domineering, arrogant, dictatorial, overbearing, despotic male chauvinist!

'Do you imagine you've married some kind of cretin? If I *did* want to go back to Boston I'm quite capable of travelling there on my own. *I do not need a keeper.*

'But as it happens I *don't* want to go back to Boston. In fact I've no intention of going back to Boston—either alone or accompanied. I'm staying here, where I belong. Wild horses wouldn't drag me away!'

Nick's face was cold and hard, the chiselled outlines stark. He appeared unmoved by Raine's outburst, except that a little tic jumped betrayingly in his jaw.

Getting her second wind and well into her stride, she went on with scarcely a pause, 'It was *you* who insisted on a honeymoon, and now because of a few cracked ribs you're afraid your macho image might be tarnished and you're trying to chicken out. Well, a wife's place is by her husband's side...' With deliberate provocation, she added, 'Even if he *is* virtually useless....'

An instant later the latch clicked and Finn was back. 'Take-off conditions seem to be fine.' He spoke cheerily, but Raine noted that his glance was wary.

Jumping in with both feet, she announced firmly, 'I won't be leaving with you, after all.' Then, apologetically, 'I'm afraid waiting for me must have held you up.'

'Think nothing of it,' Finn said, then added with a grin, 'I told the silly so-and-so you wouldn't want to leave. But after such a trauma he thought you would prefer to go.'

Looking Nick in the eye, her very glance a challenge, Raine said shortly, 'Well, I wouldn't.'

He put his good arm around her shoulders. 'So be it, my

darling. I just hope you don't change your mind after Finn has gone.'

Though shaken by the subtle but unmistakable threat, she said serenely, 'I'm sure I won't.'

'In that case—' Finn picked up his grip '—I'll be getting on my way.'

Suddenly scared, Raine asked, 'Can't you stay the night?'

'God forbid,' he said piously. 'Two's company, three's a crowd. Especially on honeymoon. But when you're back in England I may drop in for a visit, if you'll have me.'

'We'll be delighted,' Raine assured him with genuine warmth. And thought, Oh, lucky Margo, as she jumped up to give him an impulsive hug.

'Perhaps you could help your decrepit husband up?' Nick suggested, with a glint in his eye that showed his male ego had been wounded by her earlier provocative remark.

She gave him her hand and helped to haul him to his feet.

He wrung Finn's hand and clapped him on the shoulder. 'We'll look forward to seeing you as soon as you can make it.'

They walked outside and, with Nick's arm around her waist, stood together in the afternoon sunlight to wave Finn off.

By the time the small plane had disappeared over the trees Raine felt chilled through and through, but only part of it was due to the crisp air.

Beneath Nick's cool veneer she could feel the build-up of white-hot anger waiting to erupt, and knew that when they got inside she was going to have to pay for her rebellion. She began to shiver.

Feeling the uncontrollable tremors, Nick glanced down at her. 'Cold?' he asked, with mock solicitude. 'Well, let's go in and see what we can do to warm you.'

She looked up at him quickly. His expression was bland,

his eyes half closed as though in contemplation, only the steely glitter from behind the thick gold-tipped lashes giving clear warning of the retribution to come.

Having ushered her inside, he closed the door and with deliberation pushed home the bolt.

'Why are you bolting the door in the middle of the afternoon?' Despite all her efforts, she was aware that she sounded scared, breathless.

'Just to ensure our privacy.'

'Not to keep me in?'

His smile mocking, he said, 'I doubt if a single bolt could do that. You've shown yourself to be extremely resourceful, my darling. In any case, you *chose* to stay, remember?'

Grasping her arm, his fingers cruel, he propelled her towards the big settee. With a swift movement she was unprepared for he pushed her onto it so that she was half lying against the cushions and then sat on the edge, effectively trapping her there.

His good hand cupped the nape of her neck, his fingers massaging gently at first. Suddenly they tangled in the silky black hair, dragging her head back so he could see into her face. The pain made her eyes fill with water. As though the sight of her tears affected him strongly, he began to kiss her.

There was no caring in his kiss, no passion, even, but with a deliberate use of male strength to subdue female his mouth ravaged hers without tenderness or mercy until she was dazed and gasping for breath.

A moment later he had freed her mouth and pulled the cushions from behind her so that she was lying almost flat.

His face cold and calculating, his fingers purposeful, he slowly unfastened the buttons on her blouse and pulled it free of her skirt. When he'd released the front clip of her low-cut bra he pushed both garments aside to expose her creamy breasts to his gaze.

He didn't touch her, but his smile was cruel, as though he was planning what he might do to her.

It was, she realised, a calculated attempt to intimidate her, and her heart began to race at suffocating speed.

With the same care he unfastened her skirt and, grasping the hem, pulled both it and her half-slip off in one swift, ruthless movement, leaving her clad only in her dainty panties.

A single finger followed the slight dip over her flat stomach and the high-cut legs, before it began to mark the lacy pattern. She lay quite still, scarcely breathing during that leisurely, sensual tracing of every curve and contour.

When he pulled the panties down over her long slim legs and discarded them, she still made no move.

Slowly, analytically, he began to explore the flesh he'd laid bare. Repelled by his coldly impersonal examination, frightened by her own helpless reaction to it, she tried to push his hand away. His response was instant and brutal, making her freeze.

Softly, he warned, 'Yes, you'd better lie quite still, my darling. Unless you *want* me to hurt you.'

All at once she was terrified of his cold, sadistic anger. Turning her face away, she whispered, 'Please, Nick, don't do this to me...'

He wrenched her chin round and looked into her eyes, a searching, penetrating assessment. 'Are you sorry you didn't leave with Finn?'

Instinctively she knew that if she would admit she *was* sorry, admit she hated him, he would let her go.

She fought her fear and won. 'No, I'm not sorry,' she said through swollen lips. 'I wanted to stay.'

His sudden move made her flinch away, but instead of striking her, as she'd half expected, he tore off his sling and threw it aside.

'Oh, don't! Don't!' she cried, terrified that he'd hurt himself more than her. 'I won't struggle... I'll do what you want... Anything you want...'

His face becoming a taut mask, he said with a kind of savage self-contempt, 'Because you're frightened to death of me.'

She wanted to say, Because I love you. But, knowing this wasn't the right time, she said instead, 'Because I'm your wife, and I want to make love with you.'

'Are you sure you wouldn't find it too *degrading*?' he demanded bitterly, and walked away.

There was a jingle and then the noise of metal skittering across wood. A moment later she heard the bolt pulled back and the door bang shut behind him.

Hands shaking so much they could hardly complete their task, she began to pull on her clothes.

She was heading for the kitchen to make herself some coffee when she noticed the Cherokee's keys and a forest map lying by the remains of the picnic.

A second chance, she thought wryly, and left them there. She was going to stay and fight for some happiness, however brief.

When she'd drunk her coffee and tidied things away, with determination, but not without qualms, she went through to the bedroom and stripped the bed, thrusting pillows, duvet and all into a cupboard before starting to make preparations for the evening meal.

Trying not to worry when it began to get dark, she told herself sturdily that Nick knew this area like the back of his hand, and wouldn't come to any harm.

All the same, because of his injuries, her anxieties persisted, and it was a great relief when she finally heard his steps on the porch.

Curled in an armchair in front of the stove, she hadn't bothered to light any of the lamps, and he came into the shadowy firelit room with some urgency, calling, 'Raine?'

When she answered, he muttered something half under his breath that sounded like, 'Thank God,' before demanding, 'Why the *devil* are you sitting in the dark?'

'I like looking into the fire.'

She heard the rattle of a matchbox and a moment later the first of the gas-lights banished the rosy glow of the stove. As he moved to light the others she saw that he looked upset.

It took her a moment to realise that because there'd been no lights, and the Cherokee was still there, he thought something had happened to her.

Mildly, she remarked, 'I told you I wasn't suicidal.' Then, before he could make any response, 'There's a casserole in the oven if you're ready to eat.'

'Raine, I—' he began heavily.

'I don't know about you,' she broke in, deliberately making her tone brisk and bright, 'but I'm ravenous.' She knew instinctively that she'd thrown him. Whatever he'd expected, it hadn't been this cheerful normality.

He looked tired and somehow defeated, she thought, with lines of strain and bitterness etched sharply on his face. With a pang she realised that she wasn't the only one who had suffered. He'd had his share of grief and pain. The woman he loved had died, and the woman he wanted had almost killed them both in her efforts to leave him.

They ate in silence, Raine's attempts at light conversation ending in failure.

As soon as the coffee was finished, he said shortly, 'I think we could both use an early night. If you want to shower first...?'

Disappointed, because she had hoped they would sit by the fire and she'd have a chance to talk to him, she collected her night things and went into the bathroom.

When she emerged, tightening the sash of her dressing gown, he was standing staring morosely into the flames, unconsciously nursing his elbow as though his injured shoulder hurt him.

Resisting the urge to go over and put her arms around him, she said brightly, 'Your turn,' and watched him disappear without a word.

Instead of getting into bed, she went to sit by the stove, curling her slippered feet beneath her.

He returned some ten minutes later wearing one of the towelling robes, his thick blond hair still damp, his feet bare.

Turning off the main lights, leaving only the one closest to the bed, he padded over to the door and bolted it before asking curtly, 'Do you want me to make up the stove?'

She shook her head. 'I'm not tired. I'd like to sit here a bit longer.'

Instead of joining her, he headed for the bedroom door and closed it behind him. It opened again almost immediately and he came out, his mouth a tight line. Grimly, he demanded, 'Are you trying to see how far you can push me?'

She lifted innocent green eyes. 'Of course not.'

'Well, you're certainly asking for trouble.'

She shook her head. 'I'm only asking for a chance to show you how I feel.'

His teeth snapped. 'I can do without gratitude.'

'That's good, because you're not going to get any. You saved my life but I returned the favour, so as far as I'm concerned, we're even. I don't owe you a thing… And what's so wrong with wanting to sleep with my own husband?'

'Just forty-eight hours ago you said that being my wife would degrade you… Are you trying to tell me the creek incident has nothing to do with your volte-face?'

'No,' she said slowly, 'it has quite a lot to do with it. It's made me realise that life's too short to waste, that I need to seize what happiness I can, while I can. You want me, and I—'

'You're wrong. I *don't* want you.' The words were like slivers of ice.

For a moment she was shaken, then she challenged boldly, 'I don't believe you. If you didn't want me, why did you force me to marry you?'

'Perhaps it's time I showed you this.' He crossed to the wardrobe and returned with the sealed envelope she'd found in his pocket.

Her fingers suddenly unsteady, she tore it open and, unfolding the pages, recognised with surprise her father's sprawling lopsided scrawl.

My dear girl,
Now you know the truth—Nick promised he would tell you everything when the time was right. I hope you don't blame me too much for forcing your hand.

Sorry I left things so late. I kept hoping against hope that you would see what Kevin was really like, and break the engagement of your own accord. When you didn't, I started to rack my brains to find some way of ending it. I was scared stiff that too much open opposition would only serve to strengthen your determination. You can be pretty stubborn.

The action Nick and I finally agreed on was drastic, and could have misfired. But by that time I was desperate. I would never have forgiven myself if I'd let you ruin your life by marrying a man you didn't love.

I insisted on Nick bringing this letter so I could make it clear that the idea was mine, and he was a reluctant participant. Though he wanted the end result, he didn't like the means. I think he was afraid it would make you hate him.

Some time ago he told me what happened last autumn. He also told me other things, which I'm sure he's since told you...

I would have explained about Tina myself, only Nick forbade me to. He wanted you to trust him, and your refusal to even listen to him tore him apart.

He has his own kind of stubborn pride, and he's not a man to beg. I always knew that if you loved him it would have to be *you* who surrendered. But I was sure that if he'd managed to seduce you, you *must* love him.

It wasn't until I saw you in your wedding dress and you started quoting *The Lady of Shalott* that I had the slightest doubt. Happily that doubt was set at rest when you told me you did love him and always had.

All I ever wanted was your happiness, girl. I know Nick loves you, and I'm certain he's the man to make you happy.

God bless. Dad.

Dazed, Raine had to read it through twice before its meaning became clear. Oh, Dad! she cried silently, unable to find it in her heart to blame him. He'd always protected her, and he'd been trying to protect her from what he'd seen as the worst threat of all—a sterile, joyless marriage.

Looking up, she saw Nick watching her. He was standing with his back to the stove, his face in shadow, and she was unable to read his expression.

Slowly, she asked, 'The action you and Dad finally agreed on…what exactly was it?'

'Doesn't he say?'

'Not in so many words.'

'Well, I agreed to pretend that I'd bankrupt him if you didn't marry me.'

'Then you didn't put any money into Dad's firm?'

'Some. Certainly not enough to take it over, even if I'd wanted to.'

'And you don't own White Ladies?'

'No.'

Still struggling to take it in, she demanded, 'Why on earth did you agree to such a crazy scheme?'

'Your father was at his wits' end, and I didn't want to see you married to—' He broke off. Then, taking a deep breath, went on, 'Now that it's too late I know I should have heeded my own doubts and had nothing to do with it.'

'If you hadn't I would have married Kevin.'

Nick laughed harshly. 'Surely from your point of view that would have been the lesser of two evils?'

'I don't think so. Perhaps I prefer living dangerously.'

With a hint of dark colour lying along his hard cheekbones, he admitted, 'You seem to have the ability to get through my guard and make me say and do things that afterwards I'm ashamed of.'

Running a hand through his thick fair hair, he added wearily, 'I'm sorry, Raine. I never intended to hurt you, and all the time I kept hoping that somehow—miraculously—things would come right between us...'

Abruptly he turned away, and, throwing a couple of logs on the stove, said with finality, 'Now I think you should get to bed.'

With a sinking heart, she asked, 'Aren't you coming?'

'I'll stretch out on the couch.'

'And then what?'

'If you don't mind driving, we can start out for Boston tomorrow morning and be back in England the day after.'

'And then what?' she asked again.

'As soon as I've had a talk with your father, I'll return to the States and let you get on with your life.'

Struggling to keep her voice level, she asked, 'Isn't Dad relying on you to run things for a while? Or was that just part of the plot?'

'No, it wasn't. He's been talking about early retirement and having leisure enough to take up golf... But even if he changes his mind now he could do with someone to shoulder the burden—for the time being, at least. Of course he'll have *you*. And maybe Finn wouldn't object to a spell in England...'

'I don't think I want to go back to work full-time,' she said slowly. 'I'd rather like to be a wife and mother. I want children while I'm still young enough to enjoy them...'

She saw his big body tense and the hand by his side clench.

Deliberately, she added, 'I want a man I can be happy with.'

A log settled, and in the sudden flare Raine caught the flash of something akin to anguish crossing his face.

Tightly, he said, 'Then the best thing I can do is give you a divorce as soon as it can be arranged.'

Taking heart from that look, she objected. 'Dad doesn't seem to think so. Would you like to read what he says?'

She passed Nick the letter and watched while he read it. When he finally looked up, she said steadily, 'I don't want a divorce. I agree with Dad.'

'Don't be a fool,' he said roughly. 'For a lifetime's commitment you need more than just a strong physical attraction.'

'There *is* more. I love you. I told Dad so.'

'You could hardly upset him by telling him truth.'

'That *was* the truth. I fell in love with you the first time I saw you, and I've never stopped loving you.'

He half shook his head. 'When I thought I might have reason to hope, and I asked you if you loved me, you said "*Love* you? I *loathe* you! If you were up to your neck in quicksand I wouldn't lift a finger to help—in fact I'd stand and cheer while you went under."'

'I didn't mean it. Of course I didn't mean it. But I couldn't admit to loving a man I believed just wanted to use me.'

She stood up and went to him, and, both hands gripping his towelling robe, looked into his face. 'When you were in the creek, I knew that if you died I wanted to die with you.'

There was no doubting her absolute sincerity.

He made an inarticulate sound and held her close, cradling her head to his chest with such passionate tenderness that tears forced themselves from beneath her closed lids and trickled down her face.

When they drew apart a little, he wiped her wet cheeks with his fingers. 'I couldn't bear the thought of you mar rying Somersby… Though if he'd been a different kind of man and I'd been reasonably sure you loved him I would have stayed out of your life. I *did* stay out of it until it was almost too late…

'And then I was plagued by the fear that I might be making a terrible mistake. Not in breaking up your engagement, but in forcing you to marry me. You told me so many times that you hated me… I tried to kid myself you didn't really mean it, but—'

'I didn't. Oh, I *tried* to hate you—I *wanted* to hate you for making love to me when you were engaged to another woman…'

'Poor Tina,' he said softly. 'She was—'

Raine put a finger against the warm, hard line of his mouth. 'I don't need to know about Tina. It's all in the past. The only thing I need to know is that you love me now.'

He kissed the finger that lay against his lips, and then, taking her hand, pressed a kiss into the palm. 'I do love you, my heart's darling, and I loved you then.'

Sitting down, he gathered her onto his lap, encircling her with his good arm. 'Thank you for saying you don't need to know about Tina, but I *want* to tell you. Tina—or Kristina, to give her her full name—was Finn's sister…'

So *that* was why Finn's smile had seemed familiar, Raine thought.

'She was three years younger than Finn, and the three of us were more or less brought up together. I always thought of her as a sister, but at about sixteen she suddenly became shy with me. Finn told me it was a bad case of hero-worship, and pulled my leg about it.

'By the time I left college it had passed. Or at least I thought it had passed. It was only much later that I discovered she still felt the same about me. She'd just learnt to hide it better.

'I told you the Andersons were killed in an accident?'

Against his shoulder, Raine nodded.

'Well, shortly after that Tina became ill. Early tests suggested a rare and virulent form of cancer.

'Finn tried to keep it from her. Losing her parents had already knocked the stuffing out of her, and if the next lot of tests proved positive the only treatment they could offer was both painful and distressing.

'Knowing she'd been carrying a torch for me all those years, he asked me if I could give her some incentive to fight. There was no woman in my life that meant anything to me, so I asked her to marry me. And the day before she was due to go to New York to stay with an old schoolfriend we went out and bought an engagement ring.

'Such is the contrariness of fate that *you* turned up a few days later, and I knew you were the woman I'd been waiting for. I made up my mind that if the next lot of tests were negative, then I'd tell Tina about you and ask her to release me. I didn't dare think what I'd do if they were positive.

'When I invited you to go to Maine with me, I swear I didn't intend to seduce you, but you have the ability to drive me wild and make me lose my self-control… I knew I had to tell you the truth, but I was terrified of what your reaction might be and I kept on putting it off.

'Then, because Tina came home a day early, you found out before I got back from the office and ran. I arrived at the airport ten minutes after your plane had taken off.

'Unknown to either Finn or myself, Tina had been having further tests done at a New York clinic. When she told me I felt bad about not being with her, but she'd deliberately planned it that way. She didn't want fuss or pity.'

He was speaking calmly, dispassionately, his voice carefully devoid of emotion.

'I couldn't just walk out on her without knowing the results of the tests, so I waited. When the results came back, forty-eight hours later, they were positive.

'Knowing what that meant, Tina offered me my ring back. I refused to take it. But you'll never know how tempted I was. I wanted to follow you back to England and marry you immediately. But I owed the Andersons such a debt of gratitude, and in the circumstances I couldn't let either Finn or Tina down.

'Within a month she was in hospital. Though she fought every step of the way, she never came out again. But neither Finn nor I ever saw her miserable. She always had a smile.

'We were married by her hospital bed, and she died a few days later. The last thing she said to me was, "I realise how much I've had, how lucky I've been. A loving family, a super brother, and you... Thank you for making these last months so happy. When I'm gone I want you to find yourself a woman who'll make you just as happy for the rest of your life". Then, almost as if she knew, she added, "Someone like your cousin."

'But when I'd let enough time pass to be able to come to you, you were engaged, and I knew I didn't have the right to disrupt your life.'

His arm tightened. 'Don't cry, my love... Finn would be *outraged.* He believes that life should be a salute to love and courage. A joyful celebration. And that's what I intend our life together to be like.'

Slyly, he added, 'It's a pity I'm *virtually useless*, otherwise I could have given you a demonstration of how things will be...'

'Perhaps with a bit of co-operation...?' she suggested.

'Well, if I can manage to hobble to the bed...'

When they were lying together beneath the light warmth of the duvet, her palm against the slight roughness of his cheek, she leant over to kiss him.

'Raine...?'

'Mmm...?'

'Be gentle with me.'

Her little choke of laughter turned into a squeak as, with a push of his good arm, he reversed their positions. 'But first, for my own satisfaction, I'm about to show you that as husbands go I'm not quite as decrepit as you had me figured.'

And he did. To their mutual satisfaction.

Coming Next Month

THE BEST HAS JUST GOTTEN BETTER!

#2025 THE PERFECT LOVER Penny Jordan
(A Perfect Family)
While recovering from the emotional blow of unrequited love, Louise Crighton had rebounded into Gareth Simmonds's passionate arms. They'd shared a whirlwind holiday romance... but now their paths were about to cross again....

#2026 THE MILLIONAIRE'S MISTRESS Miranda Lee
(Presents Passion)
When Justine waltzed into Marcus's office, making it clear she'd do *anything* for a loan, he assumed she was just a gold-digger. He still desired her though, and she became his mistress. Then he realized how wrong he'd been....

#2027 MARRIAGE ON THE EDGE Sandra Marton
(The Barons)
Gage Baron's wife, Natalie, had just left him, and the last thing he wanted to do was go to his father's birthday party. But it was an opportunity to win back his wife; his father expected Natalie to attend the party and share Gage's bed!

#2028 THE PLAYBOY'S BABY Mary Lyons
(Expecting!)
As a successful career girl, Samantha thought she could handle a no-strings relationship with her old flame, Matthew Warner. But Sam had broken both the rules: she'd fallen in love with the sexy playboy *and* fallen pregnant!

#2029 GIORDANNI'S PROPOSAL Jacqueline Baird
Beth suspected that Italian tycoon Dex Giordanni had only asked her to marry him to settle a family score. She broke off the engagement, but Dex wasn't taking no for an answer; if she wasn't his fiancée, she'd have to be his mistress!

#2030 THE SEDUCTION GAME Sara Craven
Tara Lyndon had almost given up on men until she met gorgeous hunk Adam Barnard. Unfortunately, this perfect man also had a "perfect fiancée" waiting in the wings. There was only one thing to do to get her man: seduce him!